Her mouth thinned again to a flat white line. "You're assuming I'm going to say yes to your proposal."

Andrea picked up her left hand and stroked her empty ring finger. Her body trembled as if his touch triggered a tiny earthquake in her flesh. Touching her triggered the same in his. He could feel his blood heating with want and need. A need he would continue to ignore, because when he said it was to be a paper marriage, that was exactly what it would be. Even if he had to put his desire for her in chains. "You don't have any choice but to accept and you know it." He let her hand go and reached into the inside pocket of his jacket. He handed her a velvet ring box. "If you don't like it you can change it."

Her gaze flew from the ring box to him, eyes narrowing to slits so only her hatred shone through. "You were so *sure* I was going to accept?"

"I'm your only chance to get your hands on that money. Marry me or lose everything."

Conveniently Wed!

Conveniently wedded, passionately bedded!

Whether there's a debt to be paid, a will to be obeyed or a business to be saved...she's got no choice but to say, "I do!"

But these billionaire bridegrooms have got another think coming if they imagine marriage will be that easy...

Soon their convenient brides become the objects of inconvenient desire!

Find out what happens after the vows in:

Look out for more Conveniently Wed! stories coming soon!

Melanie Milburne

BOUND BY A
ONE-NIGHT VOW

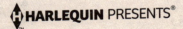

HARLEQUIN PRESENTS®

Recycling programs for this product may not exist in your area.

ISBN-13: 978-1-335-41975-0

Bound by a One-Night Vow

First North American publication 2018

Copyright © 2018 by Melanie Milburne

This edition published by arrangement with Harlequin Books S.A.

For questions and comments about the quality of this book, please contact us at CustomerService@Harlequin.com.

® and TM are trademarks of Harlequin Enterprises Limited or its corporate affiliates. Trademarks indicated with ® are registered in the United States Patent and Trademark Office, the Canadian Intellectual Property Office and in other countries.

Printed in U.S.A.

Melanie Milburne read her first Harlequin novel at the age of seventeen, in between studying for her final exams. After completing a master's degree in education, she decided to write a novel, and thus her career as a romance author was born. Melanie is an ambassador for the Australian Childhood Foundation and a keen dog lover and trainer. She enjoys long walks in the Tasmanian bush. In 2015 Melanie won the HOLT Medallion, a prestigious award honoring outstanding literary talent.

To my three doggy writing companions, Polly, Lily and Gonzo, who through the writing of this particular novel pulled me through the rough patches with their funny antics and adorable ways. xxx

CHAPTER ONE

ISABELLA BYRNE PUT down her coffee cup in the crowded café with a sigh. Husband-hunting would be so much easier if she actually wanted to get married. She. Did. Not. The thought of marrying someone was enough to bring her out in hives. Anaphylactic shock. A stroke. She wasn't the girl who'd been planning her wedding day since the age of five. She wasn't a hankering-after-the-fairy-tale fanatic like most of her friends. And now that she'd put her 'wild child' days behind her, even the thought of dating made her want to vomit.

She was Over Men.

Izzy looked at all the couples sitting at the other tables. Was no one single any more in London? Everyone had a partner. She was the only person sitting by herself.

She could have tried online dating in her find-a-husband quest, but the thought of asking a stranger was too daunting. And the small handful of friends she might have considered asking to do the job were already in committed relationships.

Izzy folded her copy of her father's will and stuffed it back in her tote bag. No matter how many times she read it, the words were exactly the same. She must be married in order to claim her inheritance. The inheritance would go to a distant relative if she didn't claim it. To a relative who had a significant gambling problem.

How could she let all that money be frittered away down the greedy gobbling mouth of a slot machine?

Izzy needed that money to buy back her late mother's ancestral home. If she failed to claim her inheritance, then the house would be lost for ever. The gorgeous Wiltshire house, where she had spent a precious few but wonderful holidays with her grandparents and her older brother before he got sick and passed away, would be sold to someone else. She couldn't bear the thought of losing the one place where she had been happy. Where she and Hamish and her mother had been happy. Truly happy. She owed it to her mother and brother's memory to get that house back.

There was twenty-four hours left before the deadline. One day to find a man willing to marry her and stay married for six months. *One flipping day.* Why hadn't she looked a little harder this month? Last month? The month before? She'd had three months to fulfil the terms of her father's will, but the thought of marrying anyone had made her procrastinate. As usual. She might have failed at school but she had First Class Honours in Procrastination.

Izzy was about to push back her chair to leave when a tall shadow fell over her. Her heart gave an extra beat...or maybe that was the double macchiato she'd had. She should never mix caffeine with despair.

'Is this seat taken?' The deep baritone with its rich and cultured Italian accent made her scalp prickle and a tingling pool of heat simmer at the base of her spine.

Izzy raised her eyes to meet the espresso-black gaze of hotel magnate, Andrea Vaccaro. Something shifted in her belly—a tumble, a tingle, a tightening.

It was impossible to look at his handsome features without her heart fluttering like rapidly shuffled cards.

Eyes that didn't just look at you—they penetrated. Seeing things they had no business seeing.

His strong, don't-mess-with-me jaw, with just the right amount of stubble, always made her think of the potent male hormones pushing those spikes of black hair out through his skin. A mouth that was firm but had a tendency to curve over a cynical smile. A mouth that made her think of long, sensual kisses and the sexy tangling of tongues...

Izzy had taught herself over the years not to show how he affected her. But while her expression was cool and composed on the outside, on the inside she was fighting a storm of unbidden, forbidden attraction. 'I'm just leaving so—'

His broad tanned hand came down on the back of the chair opposite hers. She couldn't stop staring at the ink-black hairs that ran from the back of his hand and over his strong wrist to disappear under the crisp white cuff of his shirt. How many times had she fantasised about those hands on her body? Stroking her. Caressing her. Making her feel things she shouldn't be feeling. Not for him.

Never for him.

'No time for a quick coffee with a friend?' His mouth curved over the words, showing a flash of white, perfectly aligned teeth. An I've-got-you-where-I-want-you smile that made the fine hairs on the back of her neck stand up and pirouette in panic.

Izzy suppressed a shiver and forced herself to hold his gaze. 'Friend?' She injected a double shot of scorn into her tone. 'I don't think so.'

He pulled the chair out and settled his lean athletic form into it, his long legs bumping hers under the table. She jerked her legs back as far as they would go but it wasn't fast enough to avoid the electrifying zap of contact.

Hard. Virile. Male flesh.

Izzy began to push back her chair in order to leave but one of his hands came down on hers, anchoring her to the table. Anchoring her to *him*. She snatched in a breath, the warm tensile strength of his hand making every female hormone in her body get all giggly and excited. Every cell of her body vibrated like the plucked string of a cello. She looked at his hand trapping hers and disguised a swallow. Heat travelled from her hand, along her arm and all the way to her core like a racing river of fire.

She gave him a glare so cold it could have frozen the glass of water on the table. 'Is this how you usually ask a woman to have coffee with you? By brute force?'

His thumb began a lazy stroking of the back of her hand that sent little shockwaves through her body as if a tiny firecracker had entered her bloodstream. *Pippity pop. Pippity pop. Pippity pop.* 'There was a time when you wanted more than a quick coffee with me. Remember?' The glint in his eyes intensified the searing heat travelling through her body.

Izzy wished she could forget. She wished she had temporary amnesia. Permanent amnesia. It would be worth acquiring a brain injury if she could eradicate the memory of her seduction attempt of Andrea seven years ago at one of her father's legendary boozy Christmas parties. She had been eighteen and tipsy—deliberately, dangerously, defiantly tipsy. Just like she had been at every other party of her father's. It had been the only way she could get through the nauseating performance he gave of Devoted Dad. She'd been intent on embarrassing her father because of all the behind-closed-doors torment he put her through. All the insults, the put-downs, the biting criticisms that made her feel so utterly worthless and useless.

So unloved.

So unwanted.

She'd foolishly thought: How better to embarrass her overbearing father than to sleep with his favourite protégé?

Izzy pulled her hand out from under Andrea's and rose from her seat with a screech of her chair along the floorboards. 'I have to get back to work.'

'I heard about your new job. How's that going for you?'

Izzy searched his expression for any sign of mockery. Was he teasing her about her job? Or was he just showing mild interest? There was no note of cynicism in his tone, no curl of his top lip and no mocking glint in his eyes, but even so she wondered if he, like everyone else, thought she couldn't get through a week in a new job without being fired.

But, whatever he was thinking behind that unfathomable expression, Izzy was determined not to lose her temper with Andrea in a crowded café. In the past she'd created more scenes than a Hollywood screenplay writer. But how she wanted to shove the table against his rock-hard chest. She wanted to throw the dregs of her coffee cup in his too-handsome, too-confident face. She wanted to grab the front of his snow-white business shirt until every button popped off.

How like him to doubt her when she was trying so hard to make her way in the world. To her shame, it was one of many jobs she had won and lost over the years. Her reputation always got in the way. Always. Everyone expected her to fail and so what did she do?

She failed.

She had found it hard to settle on a career because of her lack of academic qualifications. She had bombed out during her exams, unable to cope with the pressure of trying to measure up to the academic standard of her older brother, Hamish. She hadn't been one of those people who always knew what they wanted to be when they grew up. Instead she'd drifted and dreamed and dawdled.

But now she was clawing her way back, studying for a degree in Social Work online and with her job at the antiques store. Which made her all the more furious at Andrea for assuming she was lazy and lacking in motivation.

Izzy kept her chin high and her eyes hard. 'I'm surprised you haven't come in to the shop by now and bought some hideously expensive relic to prove what a filthy-rich man you are.'

His lazy smile tilted a little further. 'I have my eye on something far more priceless.'

She snatched up her tote bag from the floor and hoisted it over her shoulder, sending him another glare that threatened to wilt the single red rose on the table. 'Nice seeing you, Andrea.' Sarcasm was her second language and she was fluent in it.

Izzy wove her way through the sea of chairs to pay for her coffee at the counter but, before she could take out her purse, Andrea came up behind her and handed the assistant a note. 'Keep the change.'

Izzy mentally rolled her eyes at the way the young female assistant was practically swooning behind the counter. Not at the size of Andrea's tip—although it had been more than generous—but from the mega-charming smile he gave the young woman.

Was there a woman on the planet who could resist that bone-melting smile?

Izzy was conscious of him standing just behind her. He was so close she could feel the warmth of his body. Too close. So close she could feel electric energy fizzing along every knob of her backbone.

His energy.

His *sexual* energy.

She could smell his aftershave—a subtle blend of lemon and lime and something fresh and woodsy that made her think of a sun-warmed citrus orchard fringed by a dark, dangerously dense forest. She allowed herself a little moment of wondering what it would be like to lean back against him. To feel his muscled arms go around her, to feel his pelvis brush against the cheeks of her bottom. She imagined how it would feel to have his large hands settle on her hips and draw her nearer…to feel the surge of his hard, virile male flesh between her legs…

Oh, God. She had to stop this fantasy stuff or she would be doing a *When Harry Met Sally* scene right here and now. Meg Ryan would have nothing on her.

Andrea took Izzy by the elbow and ushered her out of the café into the watery spring sunshine. She decided to go with him without a fuss because people were already starting to point and stare. She didn't want to be photographed with him. Associated with him. Linked to him. To be seen as yet another of his sexual conquests.

Andrea Vaccaro wasn't just a press magnet—he was press superglue. Triple-strength superglue. He was an international playboy with a turnstile on his penthouse instead of a door—the protégé of the late high-flying businessman Benedict Byrne. An Italian kid from the wrong side of the tracks who had made good due to the largesse of his well-to-do English benefactor.

Izzy wasn't so much a press magnet but a press target with a big red circle on her back marked Spoilt Trust Fund Kid. But while there was a time when she had deliberately courted their attention, and even found perverse enjoyment in its negativity, these days she preferred to be left alone. Gone were the days of stumbling out of nightclubs pretending to be drunk in order to shame her father. But unfortunately the paparazzi hadn't got that particular memo. She was still seen as a wild child whose main goal in life was to party. She only had to walk past a balloon or a streamer these days and someone would post a shot with a crude caption about her.

Andrea slid his hand down from her elbow to brush his fingers against her ringless left hand. 'Found yourself a husband yet?'

Izzy knew he was aware of every word and punctuation mark on her father's will. He had probably helped her father write it. It galled her to think of

Andrea being party to such personal information. He didn't know the true context of her relationship with her father. Benedict Byrne had been too clever to reveal the darker side of his personality to those he championed or wanted to impress. Only Izzy's mother knew and she was long dead, finally resting in peace beside Izzy's older brother, Hamish. The adored son. The perfect son Izzy had been expected to emulate—but she had never quite managed to meet her father's expectations. 'I have no intention of discussing my personal life with you. Now, if you'll excuse me, I have to—'

'I have a proposition for you.' His expression was as inscrutable as a blank computer screen but she could sense the secret operating system of his thoughts. Wicked thoughts. Dangerous thoughts. *Gulp.* Sexual thoughts.

Izzy opened and closed her hand, trying to rid herself of the sensual energy he had evoked in her flesh. She tightened her stomach muscles, hoping it would quell the restless feeling deep in her pelvis, but all it did was make her even more aware of how he made her feel. 'The answer is an emphatic I'm-only-going-to-say-this-once no.'

He gave her a sleepy-eyed smile as if he found her refusal motivating. A stimulating challenge he couldn't wait to overcome. 'Don't you want to know what I'm proposing before you say no?'

Izzy gritted her teeth, mentally apologising to her orthodontist. 'I have no interest in anything you might say to me.' *Especially if it involves the word marriage.* But would he offer to marry her? For what possible reason?

He held her gaze in a silent lock that made her heart skip a beat. Two beats. The air seemed to be tightening as if all the oxygen was being sucked out of the atmosphere, atom by atom. He was looking good. More than good. But then, he always did. Tanned and toned, with the sort of classic features you mostly only saw in men's expensive aftershave ads. The bad boy made good. His not long, not short wavy black hair was styled in a casual manner that highlighted his intelligent forehead and the strong blade of his nose. The dark slash of his eyebrows—one of them interrupted by a zigzag scar—over eyes so dense and deep a brown it was hard to tell what was pupil and what was iris. Knowing, assessing eyes fringed by thick lashes that every now and again would lower just enough for her to think…

No. No. No.

She must not think about sex and Andrea in the same sentence.

Izzy could outstare most men. She could put them in their place with a cutting look or a sharp word.

But not Andrea Vaccaro.

He was her nemesis. And, damn him to hell, he knew it.

'Have dinner with me.' It wasn't an invitation. It was a command.

Izzy raised her eyebrows like a haughty schoolmarm. 'I'd rather eat a fistful of fur balls.'

His gaze moved over every inch of her face, from her eyes to her mouth, lingering there for so long she became aware of her lips in a way she had never been before. They started tingling as if his mouth had brushed them. Heated them. Tempted them. Whenever he looked at her she thought of sex. Hot bed-wrecking, pulse-racing sex. The sort of sex she hadn't been having.

Had never had.

Izzy wasn't a virgin but neither had she had as much sex as the press had made out. She didn't even like sex. She was hopeless at it. Embarrassingly, pathetically hopeless. And the only way she could tolerate it was to get tipsy so she didn't have to think about how much she wasn't enjoying it.

Andrea's obsidian-black gaze came back to hers. 'We can discuss this out here on the street where anyone can hear or we can do it in private.'

Do it in private.

The double entendre of his words sent a shiver rolling down her spine. Images popped into her head of him *doing it* with her. His hands on her breasts, his mouth on hers, his body pumping and rocking and—

Izzy pulled away from her thoughts like someone springing back from a sudden flame. She hoped she wasn't showing any sign of how flustered she felt, but she suspected there was little Andrea Vaccaro missed. It was why he was so successful in business. He could read people. He could read situations. He was clever and calculating and tactical.

She hated how he made her feel. Hated how easily he could trigger anger or desire in her. Or both. She had no interest in repeating her foolish behaviour of the past. She was no longer that brash attention-seeking flirt. She was no longer the spoilt little rich girl acting out her inner pain and shame.

She had reinvented herself.

'I'm not doing anything with you in private, Andrea.' Izzy only realised her vocal slip when she saw the way his dark eyes gleamed. *Got you.*

'Scared of what I might say?'

Scared of what I might do. Izzy raised her chin and eyeballed him. 'Nothing you say is of the remotest interest to me.'

Something moved at the back of his eyes. A camera shutter movement before the screen came back up. 'Just dinner, Isabella.' His Italian accent caressed the four syllables of her name. He was the only person who called her by her full name. She wasn't sure if she liked it or not.

Just dinner. Could she go and see what he had to say? He had intrigued her interest, and with the clock ticking like a nuclear bomb on the deadline she would be crazy not to hear him out. But being anywhere near him unsettled her. His energy collided with hers and created something in her she wasn't sure she could control.

Wasn't sure she *wanted* to control, which was even more disturbing.

Izzy folded her arms and sent him one of her trademark bored teenager looks. 'Tell me the time and the place and I'll meet you there.'

He gave a sudden laugh that made something at the back of her knees fizz. 'Nice try.'

'I mean it, Andrea. I will only have dinner with you if I come by myself.'

The satirical gleam was back in his eyes. 'Do you usually prefer to come by yourself?'

Izzy could feel her cheeks pulsating with heat. But they weren't the only part of her body pulsating. Her feminine core gave off little pulses of lust that reverberated through her entire body. She put on her game face—the face she'd perfected during her wilful teens, the wild child seductress face. The I-don't-give-a-fig-what-you-think-about-me face. Driven by an urge she couldn't quite explain, she moistened her lips with a slow sweep of her tongue, secretly delighted by the way his eyes followed the movement.

He wasn't immune to her.

The realisation was strangely thrilling. He might not like her. He might not respect her. But he sure as hell wanted her. He had resisted her seven years ago. Resisted her easily. Made her feel foolish for trying to seduce him. He'd called her a silly spoilt child playing at grown-ups.

But *now* he wanted her.

Izzy tucked that knowledge away and gave herself a mental high five. It gave her an edge, a bit of power in a relationship that had always been tipped in his favour in the power stakes. She gave him a look through her half-lowered lashes. 'Wouldn't you like to know?'

His eyes darkened until they were black bottomless pools of male mystery. 'I'll make it my business to find out.' His voice was smooth with a base note so deep every nerve in her body trembled like a shivering leaf.

Izzy knew she was being reckless in flirting with

him. Reckless and foolish. But something about the way he interacted with her always made her feel like challenging him. Pushing him. Needling him. Peeling back the carefully constructed layers of civilised man-about-town to reveal the primal man she sensed was simmering just under the surface. 'Where shall we have dinner?'

'I've booked a table at Henri's. Eight thirty tonight.'

Izzy was annoyed she hadn't put up more of a fight. She didn't like thinking of herself as predictable. She had made a lifetime's work of being anything but. How had he known she would give in? Had he been *so* sure of her?

Maybe because there's less than twenty-four hours left on the deadline?

Argh. Don't remind me.

'Your arrogance never ceases to amaze me,' Izzy said. 'Does anyone ever say no to you and mean it?'

A smile flirted with the edges of his mouth. 'Not often.'

Izzy could well believe it. She had to get her willpower back into shape. Send it to boot camp. Pump it full of steroids or something. She couldn't allow him to manipulate her into doing what he wanted. She had to stand up to him. To show him she wasn't like the droves of women who paraded in and out of his life. She might have slipped once, but she was older and wiser now. Older and wiser and wary of allowing him any hold over her. Of allowing *any* man any hold over her. She adjusted the strap of her tote bag over her shoulder and turned to leave. 'See you later, then.'

'Isabella?'

Izzy turned back to face him, carefully keeping her features in neutral. 'Yes?'

His gaze drifted to her mouth and back to her eyes, holding them like a steely vice. 'Don't even think about not showing up.'

Izzy wondered how he could read her mind. She'd planned to leave him waiting in that restaurant to show him she wasn't going to play whatever game he had in mind. He had probably never been stood up before. It was time he was taught a lesson and she would enjoy every second of teaching him it.

But now she had to think of another plan. She couldn't show up at that restaurant and meekly agree to his 'proposal'. Couldn't. Couldn't. Couldn't. He was the last man she would ever consider marrying. For it was marriage he wanted, of that she was sure. She could see the ruthless determination in his eyes.

She was desperate, but not *that* desperate.

'Oh, I'll show up.' She gave him a smile so sugar-sweet it would have made any decent dentist reach for fluoride. 'I quite fancy a free dinner. You did say just dinner, right?'

His eyes smouldered with incendiary heat, making her insides coil and twist and tighten with need. A need she didn't want to feel. A need she had strictly forbidden herself to feel. 'Just dinner.'

Izzy turned and walked back along the street towards the antiques shop where she worked. She was conscious of Andrea's gaze following her but didn't turn back to look at him. She was quite proud of her willpower—it had made a remarkable recovery, although it had been touch and go there for a minute. But when she got to the front door of her workplace and glanced back, Andrea's tall figure had disappeared into the crowd. Why she should be feeling disappointed she didn't know. And nor should she care.

But somehow—*annoyingly*—she did.

CHAPTER TWO

'GOSH. DO YOU need a bodyguard with you when you're wearing that dress?' Izzy's flatmate, Jess, asked later that evening when she poked her head around Izzy's bedroom door.

Izzy smoothed her hands down the front of her shimmery silver mini dress that sparkled like Christmas tinsel. 'How do I look?'

'Seriously, Izzy, you have amazing legs. You should give up your job selling those dusty old antiques and be a model instead.' Jess tilted her head to one side. 'So who's your date? Anyone I know?'

'Just an acquaintance.'

Jess's eyebrows rose. 'That's a pretty impressive show of thigh for a mere acquaintance.'

Izzy picked up a tube of blood-red lipstick and smeared it over her lips and pressed them together to set it in place. She knew she would be risking press attention by being seen with Andrea dressed in such a way but this time she didn't care. It would be worth it to show him she wasn't playing by his rules. He was known for dating elegant and sophisticated women. She would be the antithesis of elegant and sophisticated dressed in this get-up. This outfit screamed *party girl out for a wild time*. 'I'm teaching my…date a lesson.'

'A lesson in what? How to look but not touch?'

Izzy recalled the firm press of Andrea's hand with a delicate shiver. She was still trying not to think about him pinning her to a bed with his body doing all sorts of wicked things to her. 'I'm teaching him not to be so arrogant.' She pulled out the large Velcro rollers she'd put in her hair to give it extra volume, and finger-combed it into a cloud of curling tresses around her shoulders.

Jess sat on the edge of Izzy's bed. 'So, who is this guy?'

Izzy glanced at her flatmate in her dressing table mirror. She had only known Jess a few months and didn't want to go into the details of her complicated relationship with Andrea. She picked up a pair of cheap dangly earrings and inserted them into her earlobes, then adjusted the front of her dress to boost her cleavage. 'Just someone my father used to know.'

Jess got off the bed and came to stand next to the dressing table mirror so she could face her. 'But isn't this the last day before the deadline on your father's will?'

Izzy wished she hadn't let slip about the will in an unguarded moment a couple of nights ago over a takeout curry and a bottle of wine. It was a little lowering to admit to her friend and flatmate that her father had wanted to punish her from the grave. Her father had known how against the institution of marriage she was. She had witnessed him over-controlling her mother like a bullying tyrant until her mother hadn't been able to decide what clothes to wear without asking him first. No way was Izzy going to allow any man that sort of power over her and especially not Andrea Vaccaro. 'Yes, but he's not a candidate.'

'Are you going to forfeit your inheritance, then?'

Izzy slipped on a collection of jangling bracelets. 'I don't want to, but what else can I do? I can't just walk out on the street and pick up someone to be my husband.'

Jess's gaze drifted over Izzy's outfit again. 'You probably could wearing that get-up.' She frowned again. 'But this guy you're meeting tonight. Why isn't he a candidate? Has he actually said no?'

Izzy picked up a slimline evening purse and popped the lipstick tube inside and snapped it shut. 'I haven't asked him. And I never will. I know what

I'm doing, Jess. I know how to handle men like Andrea Vaccaro.'

Jess's eyes went as wide as the make-up compact on the dressing table. 'You're going on a date with Andrea Vaccaro? *The* hotel king Andrea Vaccaro? And you think he's not a candidate? Are you out of your mind? That man is the world's most eligible bachelor.'

Izzy scooped up a leather biker jacket from the bed and fed her arms through the sleeves, pulling her hair out of the back of the collar and settling it back around her shoulders. 'He might be considered a prize catch but I don't want him. I would rather rummage through rubbish bins and sleep under cardboard for the rest of my life than marry that arrogant, up-himself jerk.'

Jess's brows disappeared under her fringe. 'Wow. I've never seen so you…so worked up. Did something happen between you two in the past?'

Izzy did a final adjustment of her outfit. 'He thinks he can have anyone he wants but he can't have me.' She smiled a confident smile. 'Don't worry. I know *exactly* how to handle him.'

Andrea hadn't planned on being late for his dinner date with Isabella but he got caught up in traffic after a minor accident in central London. He'd sent her a text to tell her he would be a few minutes late but she hadn't replied. Her attitude towards him was exactly the reason he was going to offer her a temporary marriage. He needed a wife. A temporary wife who wouldn't make a fuss when he called it quits. No love-you-for-ever promises. No happy-ever-after. What he wanted was a six-month contract that would conveniently solve two problems with one brief, impersonal ceremony.

The teenage stepdaughter of an important business colleague was making things difficult for him by making no secret of her crush on him. The hotel merger he was working on would be jeopardised if he didn't take preventative action. And because Andrea had been asked to be best man at the businessman's upcoming wedding in a few weeks, he had to do something, and do it fast.

If it had been any other business deal he would have walked away without a qualm. There were plenty of other hotels he could buy. But this one was the one he wanted the most. Buying the hotel he'd once hung outside of as a homeless teenager looking for scraps of food made it too important to walk away. Buying that hotel in Florence—more than any other he'd bought or would buy in the future—would signify he had moved on from his difficult past.

Moved on and triumphed.

A convenient wife was what he needed and Isabella Byrne was the perfect candidate.

He figured he could help Isabella with her little dilemma while sorting out his own. Marriage was not something he had ever considered for himself. He had personally witnessed the human destruction when a match made in heaven turned into a hell on earth. He admired those who made it work and felt sorry for those for whom it failed. He enjoyed his freedom. He enjoyed the flexibility of moving from relationship to relationship without any lasting ties or responsibilities.

But he was prepared to sacrifice six months of his freedom because he wanted to nail that deal. And, more importantly, to prove he could still resist Isabella Byrne. He didn't want to want her. It annoyed him she still had that effect on him. It was a persistent ache he'd always tried his best to ignore. He had always kept his distance out of respect to his relationship with her father. Benedict Byrne had had his faults, but Andrea would never forget how Benedict's early help had launched him in the hotel business, allowing him to put his disadvantaged past well and truly behind him. He had worked hard to build an empire even bigger than Benedict's. An empire that more than made up for the miserable months he'd spent living as a street kid. No one looking at him now would ever associate him with that starving and shivering youth who had fought so hard to survive a childhood of poverty and neglect.

But now his mentor was dead, Andrea figured a short-term marriage to settle the terms of Isabella's father's will would also give him the chance to prove once and for all he no longer suffered from the Isabella itch. The itch that had been driving him mad for the last seven years.

For as long as he'd known her she'd been acting out, bringing shame to her long-suffering father. She'd been the typical trust fund kid—spoilt, overindulged, lazy and irresponsible. Not much had changed now she was an adult. She was still wilful and defiant, with a body made for sin.

He couldn't be in the same country as her without going hard. It irritated the hell out of him that she had that effect on him. He was no stranger to lust—he enjoyed a satisfying and active sex life. But something about the attraction he felt for Isabella unnerved him. Her feminine power over him was unlike any he'd felt before. He prided himself on his ability to control his primal urges. He had boundaries he skirted around but never crossed. It would be dangerous to compromise those boundaries by marrying her, but just this once he was prepared to risk it. He would insist on a paper marriage. A hands-off affair that would give them both what they wanted.

She had less than twenty-four hours left to find a husband. He'd spent the last three months bracing himself for the announcement of her engagement to some man she'd somehow managed to convince to marry her.

But she hadn't found anyone.

Or maybe she hadn't wanted to.

Not because she didn't want the money. Andrea knew she wanted that money more than anything. How else was she going to fund her lifestyle? She had an appalling employment record. The longest she'd held down a job was a month. But as much as she wanted that money, she wanted him as her husband even less. Or so she said. She would have no choice but to marry him and she knew it, which was why he'd already sorted out the paperwork. They would be married by morning or she would lose every penny of her inheritance.

And once his ring was on her finger, and hers on his, he would be off the market, so to speak, so his business deal would be safe.

Andrea saw her as soon as he walked into the restaurant. His body had sensed her three blocks away. She was sitting in the bar area, looking like a teenage boy's fantasy in a skin-tight silver lamé mini dress that showed the creamy length of her slim legs. She had big hair and more make-up and flashy jewellery than a drag queen. He couldn't help a secret smile. She knew she would have to accept his proposal, but she was making it as uncomfortable as possible for him. Did she think her wild child party girl outfit was going to put him off?

She was twirling the little colourful umbrella in her cocktail but she turned on her stool as if she had sensed his arrival. Or his arousal. Or both.

Her eyes sparkled with her usual defiance. 'You're late.'

He perched on the stool next to her, fighting the urge to stroke a hand down the slim curve of her thigh. 'I sent you a text.'

Her chin came up and something about the tight set of her mouth made him want to loosen it with a slow, sensual stroke of his tongue. 'I don't like to be kept waiting.' The words came out as cold and hard as ice cubes.

'Understandable since you've so little time left in which to find yourself a husband.' He hooked one eyebrow upwards. 'Unless you've been lucky enough to find one in the last couple of hours?'

Her glare was as arctic as her voice, making him wonder if he was going to get out of this without serious frostbite. 'Not yet, but I haven't given up hope.'

Andrea picked up a loose curl of her hair and twirled it around his finger, holding her gaze with his. She didn't pull away but her throat moved up and down over a small swallow and her pupils widened like spreading pools of ink. He could smell the exotic notes of her perfume—frangipani and musk and something that was unique to her. He carefully tucked the tendril of hair behind her ear and smiled. 'So, here we are on our first date.'

Her eyes flashed as if something exploded behind her irises. 'First and last.' She turned on her stool and picked up her cocktail glass and took a large sip. She put it down on the bar with a little clatter. 'You'd better say what you came here to say and be done with it.'

'I like your outfit.' Andrea dipped his gaze to the delicious shadow of her cleavage. 'I haven't seen this much of you in years.'

Her cheeks darkened into twin pools of pink and her mouth tightened until her full lips all but disappeared. 'I thought it'd be appropriate, given what I suspect you're going to say to me.'

He stroked a finger along the back of her hand, the base of his spine tingling when he saw his darker skin against her creamy whiteness. He could resist her. Sure he could. But he couldn't stop imagining her silky-smooth legs wrapped around his, her soft mouth beneath his own. His aching need driving into her warm, wet womanhood and taking them both to oblivion. 'You need me, Isabella. Go on. Admit it. You need me so bad.'

She snatched her hand away and used her index finger to poke him in the chest, each word like a heavy punctuation mark. 'I. Do. Not. Need. You.'

Andrea captured her hand and brought it up close to his mouth, pressing a kiss to the back of her knuckles. 'Marry me.'

Green and blue chips of ice glittered in her gaze and the muscles in her hand contracted as if his touch burned. 'Go fry in hell.'

He tightened his hold on her hand. 'You'll lose everything if you don't find a husband by morning. Think about it, Isabella. That's a heck of a lot of money to forfeit for the sake of six months living as my wife.'

He could see the indecision on her face—the doubts, the fears, the calculations. She had grown up surrounded by wealth. She had wanted for nothing but seemingly had been grateful for nothing. She had wasted the education her father had paid for by getting expelled numerous times for rebellious behaviour and poor academic performance. She had frittered away or sabotaged all the opportunities her father had provided. She acted like a selfish and sulky spoilt brat who had expected to inherit her father's entire estate without doing anything to earn it. It was no wonder she hadn't been able to find a husband willing to marry her. Her reputation was of a hell-raiser who deliberately drew negative attention to herself.

But lately Andrea had often wondered if there was more to Izzy than met the press's eye. It was like she *wanted* people to think the worst of her. She took no steps to counter the negative opinions written about her in the media. It was like she was playing a role, just as she had done this evening, dressing in an eye-popping outfit that made her look like a wild child out on the town. But in spite of her garish look-at-me clothes and make-up, he could see tiny glimpses of insecurity in the way she carried herself when she thought he wasn't looking.

Andrea knew most people wouldn't consider her ideal wife material, but he figured any wife would be better than no wife given the urgency of his situation with his business merger and the man's upcoming wedding. Besides, he was confident he could cope with Izzy. She was like a flighty thoroughbred in need of skilful handling.

And when it came to handling women, no one could say he wasn't skilful.

Her eyes suddenly hardened as if her resolve had

shown back up for duty. Her hand pulled out of his and she began rubbing it as if it was tingling. 'I can think of no worse torture than to be tied to you in marriage.'

'It will be a paper marriage.'

Her eyes widened and her mouth dropped open. 'A…a paper marriage?'

'That's what I said.'

She blinked and then blinked again, slowly, as if her eyelids were weighted. 'Do I have your word on that?'

He held her look. 'Do I have yours?'

Her mouth thinned again to a flat white line. 'You're assuming I'm going to say yes to your proposal.'

Andrea picked up her left hand and stroked her empty ring finger. Her body trembled as if his touch triggered a tiny earthquake in her flesh. Touching her triggered the same in his. He could feel himself tightening, swelling, his blood heating with want and need. A need he would continue to ignore because when he said it was to be a paper marriage, that was exactly what it would be. Even if he had to put his desire for her in chains. And a straitjacket. 'You don't have any choice but to accept and you know it.' He let her hand go and reached into the inside pocket of his jacket. He handed her a velvet ring box. 'If you don't like it you can change it.'

Her eyes flew from the ring box to his, narrowing to slits so only her hatred shone through. 'You were so *sure* I was going to accept?'

'I'm your only chance to get your hands on that money. Even if, by some chance, you found someone at this late stage, you wouldn't be able to marry without the necessary paperwork. I've seen to it. I have a lawyer and a marriage celebrant on standby. Marry me or lose everything.'

She opened the ring box and took out the diamond and sapphire ring. She spent time eyeing it, turning it this way and that. Her gaze came back to his and she gave him a tight little smile that didn't quite reach her eyes. 'You want me to wear this?'

'That's the general idea.'

She slipped off the stool, standing so close to him he could smell the fresh flowery fragrance of her hair. Her mouth was still set and her eyes as hard and blue as the diamonds and sapphires glittering in the ring. She picked up the tail of his silk tie and tugged him even closer, posting the ring down the loosened collar of his shirt. It bumped and tumbled down his chest until it lodged coldly and sharply against his stomach.

'Thanks, but no thanks.' She gave his stomach a little pat as if to emphasise her point.

Andrea captured her hand and held it against his

abdomen, every one of his muscles contracting under her touch. 'I'll give you two minutes to make up your mind and then the deal is off the table. Permanently. Understood?'

CHAPTER THREE

TWO MINUTES? IZZY could feel that clock ticking in her chest like a pin pulled on a grenade. She wanted to walk away. Wanted to slap that confident smile off his face. Wanted to poke him in the eyes and kick him in the shins and stomp on his size twelve Italian leather–clad feet.

But another part of her wanted to fish that gorgeous ring out from underneath his shirt and put it on her finger before her inheritance slipped out of her reach. For ever.

He was offering her a paper marriage but his eyes and his body were promising something else. She could feel that erotic promise thrumming in her own body. If she married him she would never have to worry about money again. She could pursue her dream of buying back her mother's childhood home and turning it into a happy place for other people, a place where families could go on holiday together during tough times, just as she and Hamish had done before he'd got cancer.

She could set herself up for life. She would no longer have to work in underpaid jobs just because she hadn't focused enough in school. Once the six months was up she would be totally free. At no one's mercy. Under no one's command.

But if she married Andrea she would be thrown into his company. Sharing his life. And yes, in spite of what he said to the contrary, sharing his bed. She could see the desire in his eyes. She could sense it in his body. She could feel it in the air when he was near her.

Could she agree to such a plan? Six months married to a man she hated and wanted in equal measure? His touch had evoked a fire in her blood that sizzled even now. He only had to look at her with those pitch-black eyes and her insides contracted and coiled and cried out loud with lust.

Izzy met his gaze and knew she couldn't possibly say no. She would have to trust him. More to the point…she would have to trust herself. He had her cornered. Trapped. She could not refuse him at this late hour and he knew it. He had it all organised. He had been so sure of her. So damn sure of her.

Why hadn't she tried harder to find someone?

Why had she let it get to this? Why had she wasted her one last chance to get away from him?

Maybe you didn't want to.

Izzy refused to listen to the prod of her conscience. She *had* wanted to get away from him. She hated him. She hated that he had received her father's love and attention, not her. He was a rich self-made man who thought he could have anyone he wanted.

Well, he was in for a big surprise because she would hold him to this paper marriage. She blew out a long breath and sat back on the stool and held out her hand. 'Okay. Give me the ring.'

His eyes held hers in a steely tussle. 'Come and get it.'

A shiver coursed down her spine at the thought of touching him again. His abs had felt like coils of concrete. And she didn't want to think about the hardness that lay just beneath them.

It was always this way between them—this tug of war of wills. She hated letting him win. It went against everything in her to allow him that much power over her. But the only way to handle him was to stand up to his challenges. Show him she was immune to him even if she wasn't and never had been. She had acted her way out of situations in the past, especially with men. Pretending to feel things she didn't. Faking it. She was an expert at fooling those she wanted to fool.

Izzy decided to brazen it out. She would prove she wasn't his for the asking. She would marry him but it would be a hands-off affair... Well, it would be once she got that wretched ring out of his shirt. She took a steadying breath and stepped between his thighs, every cell of her body intensely aware of his arrant maleness. She took the end of his tie and flipped it over his left shoulder. She undid the middle button of his shirt just above his belly button, revealing tanned muscled flesh sprinkled with jet-black hair that tickled the backs of her fingers. She undid another two buttons, breathing in the warm musky scent of him, her senses reeling like stoned bees in an opium field.

She chanced a glance at his face, her breath locking in her throat when she saw the dark satirical gleam in his eyes. His lean jaw was liberally dusted with stubble, making her want to trail her fingertips across its sexy prickliness. His hands settled on her waist and something in her stomach fell from a shelf and landed with a soft little thud that sent a shivering shockwave to her core.

'You're getting warm.' His voice was husky and low. 'Warmer.'

Izzy had to remind herself to breathe. His thighs

moved closer together, brushing against the outside of hers like the slowly closing doors of a cage. She undid another button on his shirt and dipped her hand into the opening to search for the ring. He sucked in a breath and gave a slight shiver as if her touch electrified him. She knew the feeling. The feel of his hard warm body against her hand was enough to send her ovaries into spasm. The press of his hands on her hips were melting her bones. Sending tongues of fire to her secret places. She located the ring and drew it out of his shirt and stepped back but his powerful thighs gripped her tighter.

'What are you doing?' Her voice was breathless. Too breathless. I'm-not-immune-to-you breathless.

He held out his hand for the ring, his eyes tethering hers. 'I believe it's the man's job to put the ring on his future bride's finger.'

Izzy dropped the ring into his palm before she dropped it on the floor. He slid it over her ring finger, gently but firmly pushing it into place, and gave her a smile that made something dark and dangerous glint at the back of his eyes. 'Will you marry me, Isabella?'

Izzy had never hated him more than at that moment. He was making a mockery of one of the most important questions a man could ever ask a woman. He was grinding her pride to powder. Pummelling it. Pulverising it. Relishing in the chance to over-power her.

To *control* her.

'Yes. I will marry you.' The words tasted like bile and Izzy wanted to wash her mouth out with soap. Buckets and buckets of soap.

He relaxed his thighs and she was suddenly free. Well, apart from his ring on her finger. The ring was as effective as a noose. He had her where he wanted her and there wasn't a thing she could do to stop it.

He rose from the bar stool and offered her his hand. 'We have a date with a lawyer and a mar-riage celebrant in fifteen minutes. Once that's done we can come back and have dinner to celebrate our marriage.'

Izzy glanced towards the restaurant, desperate to stall the inevitable for as long as she could. 'Don't you have to let the maître d' know to hold the table?'

Andrea's smile made something prickle across her scalp like millions of miniature marching feet. 'I've already told him.'

Izzy stood like an ice sculpture beside Andrea as the female marriage celebrant took them through the short ceremony. Five minutes before she had signed a prenuptial agreement in front of Andrea's lawyer. She hadn't minded signing...not really. Did he really think she would come after his money once their marriage was over?

She didn't want his money. She wanted hers.

Izzy tried not to think of the importance of the words they were saying to each other—the vows that were meant to be sacred and meaningful. And the fact she was dressed like a party girl while saying them. Why had she been so headstrong and stupid? She should've known he wouldn't let a silly look-at-me outfit get in the way of his plans. Anyway, why should she care she was mouthing words she didn't mean? Andrea didn't mean them either.

She tried to think of the money instead. Heaps of money that would help her finally buy back her grandparents' house and turn it into something special, something healing and special so that her mother's and Hamish's death weren't in vain. Izzy's grandparents' house had been sold after their death in a car crash not long after Hamish had died, because her father insisted on using the money to prop up his business, even though he knew Izzy's mother didn't want to sell it. Even when they were first married, her father had used her mother's wealth to build his empire and then told everyone he had done it on his own. Her mother hadn't had the strength to stand up to him. She had handed over everything—her money, her pride and her self-esteem.

But Izzy was not going to be that sort of wife—the sort of wife who said yes when she meant no. She would not bend to Andrea's will the way her mother had to her father.

She would remain strong and defiant to the bitter, inevitable end.

Andrea slipped the white-gold wedding band on her ring finger. His dark gaze seeming to say, *Mission accomplished.*

Izzy was surprised he'd been prepared to wear one himself. She placed it over his finger as instructed by the celebrant and repeated the vows in a voice that didn't sound like hers. It was too husky and whispery so she made sure her gaze counteracted it.

'I now pronounce you man and wife.' The celebrant smiled at Andrea. 'You may kiss the bride.'

Andrea dropped his hold of Izzy's hands. 'That won't be necessary.'

Izzy stared at him, desperately trying to conceal her shock. Or was it relief? No. It wasn't relief—it was rage. Red-hot rage. Why wasn't he going to kiss her? They might not have meant the vows, but surely for the sake of appearances he would have kissed her? She glanced at the celebrant but the older woman seemed unsurprised. Perhaps the celebrant had witnessed dozens of impersonal marriages and thought nothing untoward of a groom who refused to kiss his bride.

Anger curdled cold and hard and heavy in Izzy's belly—a festering, simmering stew of wrath. How dare he make a fool of her in front of the celebrant and witnesses? Damn it. She would *make* him kiss her. She softened her expression to that of a dewy-eyed bride. 'But, darling, I was so looking forward to that part of the ceremony. I know you're stuffy and uptight about public displays of affection, but surely just this once will be okay? You don't want everyone to think you don't love me, do you?'

His gaze held hers for a beat then went to her mouth and his eyes darkened to coal. His hands took hers, bringing her closer so their bodies were touching from chest to thigh. His fingers interlocked with hers in a way that contained a hint of spine-tingling eroticism. She tried to ignore the reaction in her body—the contraction of her core, the increase of her heart rate, the wings flapping sensation in her stomach. His eyes became hooded, his head bending down so his mouth was within reach of hers. She felt the warm breeze of his mint-scented breath against her lips, every nerve in her lips tingling in anticipation of his touchdown. She suddenly felt as if she would die if he didn't kiss her. Not from any sense of loss of pride, but because she needed to feel his mouth like she needed air to breathe.

His mouth connected with hers with a brush as soft as a floating feather. He lifted off but his lips were dry against her lipstick and clung to hers for an infinitesimal moment. He came back down and pressed a little harder, sealing her mouth and drawing her closer with a hand at the small of her back, the other moving up to cradle the side of her face.

Izzy had enjoyed and, yes, even endured many kisses. But nothing had ever felt like Andrea's mouth. It was electric. Exhilarating. Erotic. His lips moved against hers in a soft, exploratory way, as if he were testing and tasting the surface of her lips, storing the feel and texture of them deep in his muscle memory. She breathed in his clean male scent, her senses overloaded with sun-warmed citrus and dark, cool wood. She could feel the graze of his stubble against her face, the sexy rasp of hard male against soft female that sent a tumultuous wave of longing through her body. Even the spread of his fingers where they cradled her face made her aware of every whorl of his skin, every muscle and tendon and finger pad like her skin was reading his code.

He opened his mouth over her lower lip, stroking his tongue along its contours with such slowness, such exquisite, almost torturous slowness her legs threatened to give way. She had to cling to the front of his jacket to keep upright, pressing her body even closer. But that only made her want him more, the hungry need clawing at her, making her aware of her breasts where they were crushed so intimately against his chest, the nipples hard and tight, sensitive, aching for his touch.

She told herself she was only reacting this way because it had been so long since she'd had a lover. But she had a feeling making love with Andrea would be completely different from making love with another man. Her body recognised his touch. Reacted to it. Revelled in it. Rejoiced in it. She couldn't bear the thought of him ending the kiss. She wanted it to go on and on and on, giving her time to explore the secrets of his mouth and body, the delicious ridges and contours she could feel jutting against her body.

He sucked on her lower lip and then gently nipped at it in little tugs and releases that made her senses sing like an opera star. His tongue moved against hers in teasing little stabs that were so shockingly sexual she could feel her lower body intimately preparing itself.

Izzy heard herself whimper, those most betraying of sounds that showed she was not as immune to him as she'd wanted him to think. Her only consolation was he seemed just as undone by their kiss. She could feel the tension of his lower body, the surge of his male flesh against her, ramping up her need to an unbearable level. His breathing rate changed, so did the way he was holding her. His hand at her back pressed her more firmly against him as if he couldn't bear to let her go.

But then suddenly it was over.

He dropped his hands from her and stepped back, his expression shuttered. 'We'll lose that table if we don't get going.' His words were a slap down to her ego, making her wonder if she had imagined what had just transpired between their mouths. But then she noticed the way he ran his tongue over his lips when he thought she wasn't looking as if he was still savouring the taste of her.

Izzy followed him out of the room with her senses still spinning like circus plates on sticks. She felt dazed, drugged, disordered. Her mouth felt swollen. She could taste him on her lips. Inside her mouth. Her body was tingling from head to foot, her insides twisted and tight with unrelieved lust. For years she had wondered what it would be like to be kissed by him.

Now she knew.

But even more mortifying…she wanted him to do it again.

Izzy waited until they were inside a cab on their way back to the restaurant before she turned to look at Andrea. 'What was all that about?'

He was scrolling through his messages on his phone and didn't even glance up. 'What was all what about?' His tone sounded bored, disinterested, as if he'd been forced to share a cab with a stranger and couldn't be bothered making small talk.

She snatched his phone out of his hands and glared at him. 'Will you at least look at me when I'm talking to you?'

His expression showed no tension but she could sense it all the same. He was a master at cloaking his feelings, but something about the way he was holding his body suggested he wasn't quite as in control as he would like. 'The kiss, you mean?' His eyes drifted to her mouth as if he were remembering every pulse-racing second of when it had been crushed beneath his. His eyes came back to hers but they now had a hard sheen as if an internal screen had come up. His top lip curled over a slow but cynical smile. 'I thought we agreed our marriage was a paper one. Or are you keen to shift the goalposts?'

Izzy affected a laugh but even to her ears it didn't sound convincing—kind of like a mortician trying to be a clown. She handed him back his phone, careful not to touch him in the process. 'In your dreams, Vaccaro.'

'You will address me by my Christian name or a term of endearment when we're in public.' His voice had a note of stern authority that made her bristle like a cornered cat. 'I will not have you imply to anyone that our relationship is not a normal one. Do you understand?'

Izzy glanced at the driver, who was behind a glass soundproof screen. She turned back to look at Andrea, anger a bubbling, blistering brew in her belly. 'You think you can make me do what *you* want? Think again. You didn't marry a doormat.'

'No. I married a spoilt brat who doesn't know how to behave like a grown woman of twenty-five.' His smile had gone and in its place was a white line of tension. 'We can fight all we like in private, but in public we will behave as any other married couple who love and are committed to each other.'

Izzy folded her arms to stop herself from slapping that stern schoolmasterly expression off his face. 'And what if I don't?'

He held her gaze for a long beat. 'If either of us walks out of this marriage before the six months is up, you will be the one to lose. It's in your interests to keep me invested in this. I have much less at stake.'

Izzy frowned so hard she would have frightened off a dose of Botox. 'What exactly do you get out of this marriage? You've never actually told me your motivations.' It shamed her that she hadn't asked before now. Not that there had been much time to do so, but still. It made her look foolish and naïve. And the last thing she wanted to appear in front of him was foolish and naïve.

He slipped his phone into the inside pocket of his jacket. 'My reasons are quite simple. It suits my ends to be married for a few months.' He gave her a tight no-teeth smile that wasn't quite a smile. 'Your situation was timely. We both needed to be temporarily married and here we are.'

'But…but why me?'

He shrugged one broad shoulder. 'Better the devil you know.'

You don't know me. Izzy swallowed back the words. She didn't want him to know her… Did she? She shook off the thought and refocused. 'What do you think people are going to think of us being married? The press and so on? It's not like we've been seen together other than at some of my father's functions. And his funeral hardly counts. You barely spoke a word to me.'

'I've already informed the press.' He patted his phone in his pocket. 'They'll be waiting for us when we get back to the restaurant.'

Izzy's mouth dropped open, panic gouging a hole in her chest. 'But I can't face them dressed like this! What will everyone think?'

His smile had a hint of malice. 'You should have thought of that before.'

She sat forward on her seat and tapped at the glass separating the driver from the back. 'Pull over, please.'

The uniformed driver looked to Andrea for verification. 'Sir?'

'Drive on,' Andrea said, leaning forward to close the panel.

'No. You will not drive on.' Izzy reached for the panel again but Andrea caught her arm. 'Let go of me. I want to get out. This is kidnap. This is abduction. This is—'

'This is the bed you made and now you'll lie on it.' His fingers were like a steel bracelet around her wrist, but his thumb found her pulse and moved over it in mesmerising little circles that made it hard for her to think. His eyes were dark—impossibly, impenetrably dark.

Izzy wet her bone-dry lips, her heart thumping as if she were having some sort of medical event. Even her legs felt woolly and useless. She couldn't do this. She couldn't allow him to make a fool of her. She would have to try another tactic. She pulled out of his hold and put a hand to her head, rubbing at her tight temples. 'Please, Andrea. Could I go home and change first? Henri's is such an upmarket restaurant.

I didn't realise tonight would end like this. It's all happened so quickly and I—'

'You've had three months to find yourself a husband.'

She steepled her hands against her nose and mouth, taking a deep calming breath. She didn't want to disgrace herself in front of him. To show how vulnerable she really was. She had to be strong. Strong and invincible, otherwise she would break and she wouldn't be able to put herself together again.

She had skated too close to the abyss before. Terrifyingly close.

She had worked hard to get herself strong again. *Must not cry. Must not cry. Must not cry.*

'I know…but I kept putting it off,' Izzy said. 'I was frightened of making a mistake…marrying the wrong man or something, one who wouldn't agree to the six-month time limit and make things even more impossible than they already are.' She lowered her hands and looked at him again. 'I mean, it's not exactly a normal situation, is it? How many fathers would do this to their only daughter? Their only remaining child?'

He studied her for a moment. 'Your father loved you but you constantly disappointed him. It grieved him terribly that you didn't make more of an effort with all the opportunities he gave you.'

Izzy closed her eyes in a slow blink and sat back heavily against her seat. 'That's me all right. One big disgusting disappointment.' She released a shuddering sigh. 'Go me.'

There was a long silence.

Andrea leaned forward again and slid open the glass panel. 'Driver. Change of plans.'

CHAPTER FOUR

ANDREA WAITED IN Izzy's sitting room while she changed her outfit. He tried not to think about their kiss at the ceremony—the kiss that had almost got out of his control. For years he'd thought about kissing her and he hadn't been one bit disappointed. Her mouth was as soft and yielding and as passionate as he'd dreamed. More so. It had been like tasting delicious nectar, finding his tastes so attuned to its sweetness he couldn't stop the desperate craving for more.

Even now he could still taste her. He could still recall the pillowy softness of her lips moving under his. Could still feel the darting flickers of her tongue and her beautiful breasts crushed against his chest. His body was aching with need—a need she had stirred in his flesh, making him feel like a horny teenager. He'd prided himself on his control and yet one press of those soft lips against his and he'd been tempted to change the terms of their agreement.

Sorely tempted.

Dangerously tempted.

Why was it Izzy who made him feel so close to the edge of his control? During that kiss he'd all but forgotten they were in a registry office in front of witnesses. His senses had been so tuned in to her, every thought had flown from his head other than how much he'd wanted her. His blood had pounded with it.

Damn it, it was still pounding.

He needed more than a cold shower. He needed an ice bath. He needed to stay in control. He wanted her, wanted her desperately, but it didn't mean he would act on it. Acting on it would complicate things. Make their relationship even trickier than it already was.

Andrea swept his gaze around the room, wondering how a young woman from such a wealthy background could live in such a cramped space. The furniture looked second-hand and, while it was shabby chic, it seemed strange she hadn't decorated in the manner to which she had been born. She had stubbornly refused to live in the Hampstead flat her father bought her for her twenty-first birthday. It was now part of her inheritance, having been rented out for the last four years.

Had this been her way to snub her father? To live like an impoverished student? But then his gaze went to a stack of textbooks on a table next to the sofa. A laptop was perched nearby. He looked at the social work titles and frowned. Did the books belong to her flatmate or was Izzy studying online? Perhaps the impoverished student atmosphere of the flat was a reality. But she'd enrolled in courses before and spectacularly failed.

Andrea had always struggled to understand her attitude to her father. While he had never considered Benedict Byrne to be a perfect father, he still didn't think Benedict had deserved how Izzy had behaved towards him. Her rebellious streak had caused her father so much shame and heartache. Her behaviour throughout her teens and early adulthood had been outrageous at times. Underage drinking, hard partying, mixing with the wrong people—all of it orchestrated to draw as much negative attention to herself as possible. Andrea found it hard to have any sympathy for her because the only father figure he'd known had been a cruel sadistic bastard of a stepfather who had beaten his mother, and when Andrea had tried to defend her he'd been kicked out on the streets.

He'd been fourteen years old.

Andrea hated thinking about his past. He was no longer that terrified boy who had no roof over his head. The boy who had been sick-to-his-guts worried about his mother, but when he came back the next day to help her escape, to his shock and despair, she had asked him to go away. Told him she didn't want him any more. His mother had chosen to stay with her violent partner rather than have Andrea help her get away. He had bled for days from the wound on his face from the backhand from his stepfather and to this day carried the scar. It was a permanent reminder of how ugly relationships could get, and how even people who you thought loved you most in the world could still turn against you when you least expected it.

If it hadn't been for Izzy's father crossing paths with Andrea a few months later, who knew what would have become of him? He had gone from begging for food outside hotels and restaurants to owning some of the most luxurious hotels in Europe. With Benedict's help he had chosen a different path, a different life, a different future.

And for the next six months that future included Izzy as his temporary wife.

Izzy came out dressed in a navy blue knee-length dress with three-quarter sleeves with velvet-covered heels to match. The colour of her outfit intensified the blue of her eyes, but a shutter had come up in her gaze, reminding him of unreachable galaxies in a midnight sky. Her mouth was shiny with lip gloss and he couldn't stop thinking about how it felt beneath his own. How she tasted. How she responded.

The fire in her had struck a match to the simmering coals of his desire.

Her gaze moved out of reach of his. 'I'm ready.'

He pointed to the books and the laptop. 'Are these yours?'

Her chin came up. 'Yes. What of it?'

'You're studying for a degree?'

Her eyes moved away from his. 'What if I am?'

'Isabella.' Andrea touched the back of her hand and she raised her gaze to meet his. He knew he should try not to touch her so much but the temptation, the need was *always* there. She was like a potent drug he couldn't summon the willpower to resist. And now he'd fed the desire to touch her by kissing her and holding her in his arms, he was going to have to work a lot harder to keep his desire under control.

She pulled her hand away as if his touch disturbed her. 'Yes?' Her voice had a coating of frost around the edges.

'It's great that you're studying. Really great.' He opened and closed his fingers to stop them from tingling from her touch. 'You're doing a Social Work degree?'

'I had to do some extra night classes to get in but I'm scraping through so far.'

'I'm sure you're doing much more than scraping

through,' Andrea said, wondering if she had failed in the past by choice rather than lack of academic ability. 'We need to talk about our living arrangements. Or, more to the point, yours.'

Her eyes widened to pools of startled blue ink. 'Pardon?'

'We will be expected to live under the same roof now that we're—'

'I'm not living with you.' She flung away to the other side of the room, spinning back around to glare at him. 'You planned this, didn't you? You tricked me into marrying you and now you're insisting on ridiculous living arrangements. I won't do it. I won't live with you.'

'I said under the same roof, not in the same bed,' Andrea said with measured cool. 'But if you change your mind I'm more than willing to see to your needs.' *What are you doing?* But he didn't want to listen to the voice of his conscience. His conscience could get the hell out of his head. He wanted Izzy and she wanted him. He could feel her desire for him like a current in the air. The same current that was moving through his body in ripples and tingles that left no part of him unaffected.

Her cheeks were fire-engine red, her hands in tight fists by her sides. 'I will not change my mind. I loathe you. You disgust me.'

'That wasn't the message I was getting when you were kissing me back at the celebrant's office.'

Her eyes flashed with vivid blue venom. '*You* kissed me.'

'You asked for it, remember? You practically begged me to—'

She picked up a scatter cushion and threw it at him but it missed and knocked over a photo frame instead. Andrea bent down to pick up the cushion and the frame, setting the frame on the lamp table and then placing the cushion back on the sofa with measured calm. 'Rule number one. No violence. Ever. Not under any circumstances.'

Her expression was a road map of resentment. 'You provoked me.'

'Doesn't matter. No amount of provocation makes it acceptable to throw something at someone, even if it's just a cushion. You have the same assurance from me. You're entitled to feel safe at all times with me. I give you that promise.'

She began to chew at her lower lip, glancing at him from beneath lowered lashes. 'Okay...but I still don't want to live with you.'

'That is not negotiable, I'm afraid,' Andrea said. 'I'll send packers to collect your things in the morning. We will spend the night in my hotel in Mayfair. Tomorrow we will fly to my villa in Positano in Italy.'

'But what about my lease here?' Her brow was troubled with a frown. 'I'll have to pay the rent even if I'm not here because my flatmate—'

'I'll settle it with your landlord and your flatmate.'

'What about my job?'

'You can hand in your notice tomorrow and concentrate on your studies instead. You'll have no need to work unless you particularly want to. Your full inheritance won't be available until the six months is up but, along with the sum your father stipulated you receive upon your marriage, I'll pay you an allowance in the meantime, a generous one, so you'll want for nothing.'

Her eyes flashed another round of fire at him. 'Except my freedom.'

'Isabella.' Andrea released a long-suffering sigh. 'Your future freedom depends on you abiding by the terms of your father's will. I'm making that possible for you so the least you can do is be grateful.'

Her plump lips thinned to a sneer. 'Would you like me to drop to my knees in front of you and demonstrate my gratitude right now?'

Andrea's groin twitched at the sultry challenge in her eyes. He considered calling her bluff. He could think of nothing he wanted more than to have his lust for her satisfied by her lush mouth and hot little tongue. Had he ever wanted a woman more than this one? She stirred in him the most primal urges—urges he could only just control when he was around her. His desire for her was growing, swelling, expanding in his blood and rocketing through his body like a virulent virus. He was hot for her. There wasn't a part of his body that didn't want her to crawl all over it and suck and lick and stroke and, yes, even to bite.

'Pack an overnight bag,' he said, doing everything in his power to keep his gaze away from her mouth. 'I'll wait in the cab.'

Izzy stuffed a few things in a bag with such anger barrelling through her system she thought the top of her head would explode. How had she allowed herself to be so blindsided by Andrea? She'd foolishly assumed they would marry and that would be it. He would go one way and she would go the other.

But no.

He wanted a wife. It *suited* him to have a wife. But why her? She was the most unsuitable wife in London. You didn't have to look too far back online to see some of the things that had been reported about her. Not all of them true, but 'once a tart, always a tart' as far as the press and the public were concerned.

Izzy hadn't done herself any favours in that regard. Deliberately inciting negative press, making her nights out clubbing look far more incriminating than they were. She had relished the shame it had brought to her father's door. She had enjoyed every cringeworthy second of her payback for all the disappointment and hurt and despair he'd inflicted.

But she hadn't been mature enough back then to realise the shame would stick like mud on her door far longer than it would on his. She couldn't apply for a job these days without someone finding an oftentimes ambiguous but no less damning shot of her on social media.

Once that stuff was online it was always online.

Why had Andrea waited until now to force her hand? Why not approach her three months ago? Why leave it until the midnight hour when all her other options were gone?

Not that she'd had any other options. And, truth be told, she hadn't looked as hard as she should have to find a husband. She'd only just enrolled in her course and juggling work and study had been more than enough to handle. She'd been so angry at the way her father had engineered things that she'd wasted two months seething. And then the sick, sinking feeling every time she thought about finding a man to marry her had made it impossible to do much other than search through the list of contacts on her phone and break out into a prickly sweat because no one was suitable or, even if they had been, they would never have been agreeable.

But, strangely, Andrea Vaccaro was agreeable. More than agreeable. He'd made it all but impossible for her to say no. He'd made sure she wouldn't be *able* to say no. He'd covered all the bases, tied up all the loose ends, ensnaring her so cleverly in his web like a spider did an unsuspecting fly. That self-congratulatory glint in his eyes at the ceremony proved how much he was enjoying having her in his power. *Grrr.* Under his command.

Izzy had never considered him as a temporary husband. Never. She'd skipped past his name in her phone as if she were avoiding contamination. Just seeing his name there had been enough to make her heart stutter and her breath stick in the walls of her throat.

But now she was wearing his ring on her finger and the only way she would be free of him was when the six-month period was up. *Six months!* Six months living with Andrea, pretending to be his wife in public.

How would she survive the torture?

Even more worrying…how would she survive the temptation?

Izzy remained silent in the cab until it pulled into the forecourt of Andrea's luxury hotel in Mayfair. The paparazzi had gathered and were waiting under the crimson and gold awning that sheltered the drive-through area in front of the grand old building. Had he given the press the heads-up? Or had they automatically assumed he would bring her here for their...*gulp*...wedding night? It was, after all, his home when he came to London. He mostly lived between his two homes in Positano and Florence. She glanced at Andrea with a frown. 'I thought we were going back to Henri's for dinner?'

'It's been a big day.' That self-satisfied gleam was back in his eyes. 'We both need an early night, *si*?'

Izzy couldn't control the shimmery little tremor that went through her body. It was as if champagne had been injected into her bloodstream—little bubbles of forbidden excitement that made her breath hitch and her heart hammer. She couldn't be alone with him until she got herself back under control. She had no defence against the pull of attraction. It was like trying to fight a bloody battle with a paper sword. 'But I was looking forward to eating at Henri's. It's one of my favourite places. I'm hungry and—'

'I'm sure I'll find something in my hotel to satisfy that appetite of yours.' Something about his tone made her suspect he might not be talking about food. 'I'll handle the press,' he added. 'And remember, we're madly in love and are now on our honeymoon.'

A hotel porter came to collect Izzy's overnight bag from the cab. Andrea led Izzy past the paparazzi, stopping long enough to say they would like some privacy to celebrate their marriage. The congratulations were hearty and enthusiastic, and some of the comments he made back to the press made it sound like Izzy had been waiting for this moment for most of her life. Sickening. Just sickening. She had never felt more furious. How dare he tell the world she'd had a crush on him since she was a teenager?

She hadn't.

She didn't.

She *never* would.

The cameras continued to flash and click like rapid gunfire, the recording devices thrust in front of their faces to such a degree Andrea put his arm up to shield Izzy's from them. 'Thank you, everyone,' he said. 'It's time for us to be left alone now to enjoy our first night together.'

Their first night together...

How those words made her insides shiver and her pulse race. His arm around her waist was a steel cord of strength but, strangely, she felt protected by it. She hadn't felt as threatened as she normally would when the press surged at her. He had made sure no one bumped her or came too close. It was nothing but an act—a charade of Loving Husband for the cameras. But, even so, it made her solid dislike of him soften a little around the edges.

Andrea took her to a private elevator that only senior hotel staff used, the doors closing off the rest of the world with a gentle swish. Izzy immediately sprang to the other side of the elevator and folded her arms across her body, shooting him a glare that was multiplied by the mirrored walls.

He leaned with indolent grace against the side wall. 'It seems we have created quite a storm of interest, *cara*.' His lazy smile came at her from every wall of the elevator. 'The heiress *enfant terrible* and the billionaire hotelier has quite a ring to it, does it not?'

Izzy ground her teeth until her molars threatened mutiny. 'Did you have to make up such absolute rubbish about me? I have not, did not and will not ever have a crush on you.'

His gaze swept over her body as if he was removing every stitch of her clothing. Heat flared between her thighs when his gaze came back to hers. Smouldering eyes. Eyes that burned holes into her resolve like laser pointers. 'You have always wanted me, *cara*. I feel it every time you look at me.'

'Right back at you, buddy.' Izzy raised her chin. 'I've seen the way you look at me. And for God's sake stop calling me *cara*.'

He pressed the emergency stop button on the elevator and it came to a gliding halt. So did Izzy's breathing. 'W-what are you doing?'

He came to where she was standing against the back wall of the elevator, stopping so close to her she felt his muscled thighs brush hers. He put one hand on either side of her head, caging her between his arms. His chocolate-brown eyes meshed with hers in a lock that made the floor of her belly shiver like tinsel in a breeze. 'I'm not denying I want you, *tesoro mio*. I want you very much. But I think you want me more, *sì*?' One of his thighs gently nudged her legs apart and she gasped when the hard ridge of his muscle-packed leg came in contact with her mound.

Izzy couldn't breathe. Her heart was beating so fast and so erratically she thought it might pop right out of her chest. Every pore of her body was aware of him—acutely, thrillingly aware. She couldn't stop staring at his mouth—the sexy masculine contours that had felt so magical against her own. She moistened her lips and he followed every millimetre of its journey with his hooded gaze. 'Other people might need to use the elevator.' Her voice was so croaky it sounded like she'd been hanging around a frog pond and got too friendly with the natives.

His smile tilted a little further, making his eyes darken even further. 'It's my hotel. My elevator. And you are my wife.'

Izzy intended to push him away but somehow her hands fisted in his shirt instead. The toned muscles of his chest were like plates of steel against her knuckles, the citrus and woodsy fragrance of him making her dizzy with longing. 'In name only.'

'So far.' He lowered his head to brush his stubbly jaw against the side of her face, sending her senses into frenzy. 'But how long will that last?'

Desire flooded her being. Giant, thumping, pumping waves of it moving through her with such force she had trouble standing. Had she ever felt lust so powerful? So overwhelming? It was like a fever in her blood, a racing, raging red-hot fever that made it impossible for her to think of anything but how he made her feel. 'I'm not going to sleep with you, Andrea.' *But I want to. I want to so badly.*

He moved his mouth to just an inch above hers, his warm breath mingling intimately with hers. His thigh moved against her, teasing the heart of her with slow rubs and nudges that made her knees wobble and her spine melt like honey in a heatwave. 'We'll be good together, *cara*. Better than good.'

Izzy's fingers gripped his shirt even tighter but still she didn't push him away. *Why aren't you pushing him away?* The alarm bell of her conscience was too faint for her to take notice. It was like trying to hear someone's whisper at a heavy metal concert.

Her need of him was too strong, too powerful. She closed the distance between their mouths, pressing her lips to his, delighting in the tantalising feel of him responding.

He took control of the kiss with a bold stroke of his tongue across her lips, entering her mouth and calling her tongue into a sexy tango that made every knob of her vertebrae tingle like fairy dust was being trickled down her spine. She pressed herself closer, linking her arms around his neck, her fingers delving into the thickness of his hair. She stretched up on tiptoe so she could feel every delicious hard ridge of him against her body, the friction revving up her desire like bellows in front of a fire. Her breasts were crushed against his chest and she was suddenly aware of their sensitivity, as if they were already anticipating the stroke of his hands, the glide of his tongue, the gentle scrape of his teeth.

She whimpered against his mouth, wanting more, needing more, aching for more. His mouth was still crushed to hers, his tongue playing with hers in a kiss that mimicked the erotic caress of his thigh against her. Sensations sparked and fizzed like fireworks in her body. Sensations she had not felt with a partner before. She could do this alone but never with a partner. She'd always had to fake it rather than admit her failure.

But Andrea had unlocked her sensuality in a way no other man had. The tension in her core grew and grew, the sensitive nerves tight and tingling. Her legs, her thighs, deep in her body the tingles ran up and down and around and around until she was unable to process thought. He increased the friction of his thigh as if he was reading every nuance of her body. She couldn't possibly be feeling like this... how could it happen so easily? How could he have so much sensual power over her to reduce her to a quivering, whimpering wanton? She gasped as the wave rose and rose inside her, the little ripples growing, swelling, burgeoning until they broke over her in a massive rush, shattering her senses into thousands of pieces like confetti fluttering through her blood.

Izzy opened her eyes and then closed them, squeezing them tight against the smug expression on Andrea's face. Oh, God, why had she allowed him to reduce her to this? To a reckless, shameless wanton who hadn't enough self-control to withstand the temptation of his touch. Why hadn't she resisted him? Where was her willpower? Damn it. Where was her pride? Why had she allowed him to prove his point with such embarrassing, devastating accuracy?

He wasn't the one who couldn't control himself.

She was. And he had proven it.

Izzy hadn't thought it possible to hate someone

so much for bringing her such amazing pleasure. If this was what his hard thigh could do to her, what on earth would making love with him be like?

Andrea lifted her chin, his eyes gleaming with triumph. 'What did I tell you? Dynamite.'

Izzy summoned what was left of her pride. She pushed him away and schooled her features into a mask of cool indifference. 'How do you know I wasn't faking it?'

He studied her for a beat or two. 'You don't have to feel ashamed of how you respond to me. It will make our marriage much more satisfying.' He pressed the button to get the elevator going again. 'For both of us.'

The doors opened on his floor and he ushered her out of the elevator with a hand at her elbow. Izzy knew she should move away from the warm, gentle cup of his hand but somehow couldn't bring herself to do it. He opened his penthouse suite with his key card and turned to her. 'Shall I carry you over the threshold?'

Izzy shot him a glare so lethal it could have blacked out the lights. 'Don't even think about it.'

CHAPTER FIVE

IZZY STEPPED INTO the suite, the sound of the door clicking shut as Andrea came in behind her making her heart give a little stumble and her legs tremble.

She was his wife.

He was her husband.

They were alone.

Inside his hotel suite.

Her body was still tingling from the shocking intimacy he had subjected her to. Intimacy she should have put a stop to but somehow hadn't. Why not? Why had she allowed him to prove how much more she needed him than he needed her? The power balance was all out of kilter.

Izzy drew in a shaky breath and glanced around the suite. The décor of the suite was stunning but not in an over-the-top way. The crystal chandeliers, ankle-deep dove-grey carpet and grey-blue velvet-covered sofas with stylish scatter cushions gave the room a welcoming, restful feel. Lamps were turned down low to give a muted glow that highlighted the private, sanctuary-like atmosphere of the suite. It was a masculine suite and yet it had softer touches such as vases of fresh flowers and cashmere throw rugs draped elegantly on each of the sofas. The curtains were the same blue-grey as the sofas and were drawn back from the windows to showcase the view.

Izzy moved through the suite, stopping to look at the artwork on the walls—originals, not prints, of course. There was a dining area off the main sitting room and the master bedroom and en suite bathroom through another door. She peered inside the master bedroom, her eyes going straight to her overnight bag positioned on the velvet-covered luggage rest. No doubt it had been delivered while she and Andrea were in the elevator. She closed the door and turned and looked at him. 'Where's the other bedroom?'

'There isn't one.' He shrugged off his jacket and laid it across the back of one of the sofas. 'You'll be sharing mine.'

Izzy's stomach dropped so far it bounced and knocked her heart into her throat. 'What? What sort of penthouse is this if it only has one bedroom?'

His expression was inscrutable. 'Is that going to be a problem for you?'

'Of course it's a problem.' She stalked as far away

from him as she could get, sending him a glare so blistering she was surprised the paint didn't peel off the walls. 'I told you I'm not sleeping with you. I want my own room.' She folded her arms and planted her feet. 'I want my own suite.'

Andrea casually loosened his tie, his gaze still meshed with hers. 'Not possible, I'm afraid.'

'But you own the flipping hotel!' Izzy's voice was so shrill she thought it might shatter the chandeliers. She knew her outraged virgin reaction could be considered a little inconsistent given her reputation, but she couldn't possibly share a bedroom with him. Sharing a bedroom meant sharing a bed. She'd shared an elevator with him and look how *that* turned out.

Andrea's tie landed alongside his jacket and he reached up to undo a couple of the buttons of his shirt. His calm demeanour and his slow and methodical movements as he released the buttons were in stark contrast to how she was feeling, which made her even more furious with him. 'Precisely,' he said, his eyes so dark her insides gave a little flutter. 'Which is why you're sharing this suite with me. I will not have my domestic staff think this is not a genuine marriage.'

Izzy began pacing the floor in case she was tempted to undo the rest of those buttons for him.

She forced her gaze away from his tanned and toned chest with its dusting of crisp masculine hair. She had to get a hold on herself. She was meant to be standing up to him, resisting him, not gawking at him like some kind of sex-starved spinster.

He was enjoying every second of her panic. He was so cool. So enviably, damnably cool. He reminded her of a cat who had cleverly cornered a mouse. He was biding his time, waiting for the perfect moment when one of his velvet-covered paws would strike his hapless prey.

There was going to be no such moment.

Izzy straightened her spine as if she were the star student at deportment school. 'If you think I'm going to get in that bed with you and allow you to touch me, think again. If you so much as lay one finger on me I will scream so loud your staff will have to replace all the chandeliers. And the windows. In the entire hotel.'

Andrea gave a low deep chuckle. 'I have no problem with a little screaming coming from my bedroom. The louder the better.'

Izzy spun away to stand stiffly in front of one of the windows. She couldn't allow him to do this to her—reduce her to a tantrum-throwing termagant. She had to act cool and unmoved by his attempt to unsettle her. She had to call his bluff. He was doing this to needle her. He knew how much she hated him. He was trying to get the upper hand in their relationship. And she was handing him free points every time she reacted like a spoilt child.

She had to think of another tactic—another way to outsmart him. *Think. Think. Think.*

Izzy took a calming breath and turned around to face him. 'All right. You win. We share the bed. But I should warn you I'm a terribly restless sleeper.'

His expression showed no apparent satisfaction that she'd changed her mind, but she couldn't help wondering what was going on behind the screen of his impenetrable gaze. 'Perhaps I can find a way to relax you, *si*?'

Izzy turned away before he saw the longing she was trying to suppress. Why was he the only man who could do this to her? Make her angry and aroused in equal measure. 'I'm going to have a shower.' She turned for the master bedroom and its en suite bathroom.

'What about dinner?'

'I'm not hungry.'

'You might change your mind after your shower,' Andrea said. 'I'll order something for you.'

Izzy closed the bedroom door by way of answer. She leaned back against it with a heavy sigh, wondering how she was going to get through a whole night sleeping beside Andrea. It was like asking a chocolate addict to spend the night in a chocolate factory. How would she stop herself from touching him? And what if he touched her? He only had to look at her to get her hot and bothered.

What had happened to her defences?

To her resolve?

She moved away from the bedroom door and went to the luxurious en suite. The bathroom was decked out in marble with the same blue-grey tones of the bedroom, teamed with a white freestanding bath and twin basins with stunning ornate silver-trimmed mirrors. Soft fluffy towels as big as blankets were on the silver towel rails and more were rolled stylishly on a glass shelf. The shower was so big it could have housed an entire football team, and it had a large square rainwater showerhead. The bathroom smelt of exotic essential oils and there were bottles of the Vaccaro signature toiletries positioned on the marble counter near the basin and more in the shower and next to the bath. Two blue-grey bathrobes hung on silver hooks on the back of the door, and Izzy couldn't help wondering who had been the last woman to spend the night with Andrea here.

Izzy stripped off her clothes and stepped under the shower, tilting her head back so the water could wash over her as if she were standing in a waterfall in a rainforest. She was no stranger to luxury. While she was growing up, her father had always insisted on staying at the best hotels because he believed a businessman of his status deserved the best. But something about Andrea's hotel had more than just over-the-top luxury. It had class. Sophistication. Understated glamour. The simplicity of design and detail hinted at a man who liked and appreciated the good things in life but was not one to flash his wealth around in a status-seeking manner.

Once she'd finished showering, Izzy dried off and dressed in her nightgown and slipped on one of the bathrobes. She roughly dried her hair using the hairdryer she found in one of the bathroom drawers and then scooped it loosely on top of her head in a makeshift ponytail. She looked at her make-up-free face and wondered if she should put on some cosmetic armour, but then decided against it. She wasn't out to impress him. What did it matter if she didn't look anything like his gorgeous and sophisticated bed buddies?

She. Did. Not. Care.

Izzy came out of the bathroom to find the suite empty apart from a dinner trolley that was set up next to the dining table off the sitting room. She did a quick search of the rest of the suite but there was no sign of Andrea. She went back to the dinner trolley and lifted the silver domes off to see if he had eaten anything but the delicious-looking food was untouched. There wasn't a note left anywhere and when she checked her phone there was no text message either. If he was so keen to keep up appearances, then why wasn't he in the suite with her?

Izzy leaned down to smell the food and momentarily closed her eyes in bliss. There was a bottle of champagne in an ice bucket, desserts under another lid, fresh fruit and a cheese plate under another. There were little savoury pastries and tartlets and some crab cakes and fresh oysters. A seafood dish that was fragrant with lemongrass and lime and chilli and coconut milk was in another dish with a bowl of fluffy jasmine rice flecked with coriander. It was a feast of her fantasies and she was suddenly so hungry she felt faint. She looked at her phone, wondering if she should call or text Andrea to see where he was but decided against it. She didn't want to start acting like a suspicious wife, checking up on his whereabouts.

Why should she care where he was?

There was a message on her phone from her flatmate, Jess, who had apparently seen something on Twitter about Izzy and Andrea's surprise marriage. It was a little shocking to realise how quickly the news had travelled. Izzy texted back to say she would be moving out but not to worry about the rent because Andrea had promised to pay out the lease. Even as she typed the words, she realised how much control she had handed to him. He was paying her bills, sorting out everything for her like she had no mind of her own.

Izzy put down her phone and sighed. She would have to suck it up because the only way she could get her grandparents' house back was to abide by the terms of her father's will. The allowance Andrea had offered to pay her would help, so too would the money her father had stipulated would be paid to her upfront upon her marriage, but the full balance would not be in her hands until the six months was up. She had already spoken to the current owners and they had graciously agreed to hold back from putting the house on the market until December. She'd had to make them an offer they couldn't refuse to get them to hold off selling but she didn't care how much it cost her.

Buying back her grandparents' house was a way to right the wrongs of the past—a way to honour her mother and her brother by bringing back what should never have been taken away.

Andrea sat in his office on the first floor of the hotel and sorted out a couple of issues his manager had brought to his attention. He knew he could have just as easily seen to them in the morning, but he felt the need to clear his head. Izzy's response to him in the elevator had made him realise the electric heat that fired between them. He became like a horny teenager when he was with her. She excited him like no other woman. There was a dangerous element to what he felt about her. The raw desire that pumped in his blood pushed him into a place he had never allowed himself to go before now.

He wanted her so badly it was all he could think about. How much he wanted to drive himself into her moist heat. How he wanted to hear her scream his name. How he wanted to feel her come apart around him.

He'd contained his lust for her for years. For years he'd thrown himself into work, pummelled the forbidden desire out of him by long punishing hours, driven himself to achieve what others only dreamed about. He had everything money could buy. He had achieved more than he had set out to achieve.

He wasn't after the happy-ever-after package. And Izzy was certainly not the woman to give it to him. Her negative attitude to marriage was his safety hatch—the escape route so that when the six months was up he could walk away without a qualm. It was a means-to-an-end marriage. A mutually satisfying arrangement that would give them both what they wanted. He'd been rethinking his paper marriage stance. Why shouldn't he indulge his desire for her and hers for him? It was clear they wanted each other. The way she'd responded to him in the elevator proved that she wasn't immune to him any more than he was to her.

She would get her inheritance and he would get her.

But Andrea was prepared to take his time about it. He wanted her to be the one to come to him. And her coming apart on his thigh in the elevator was an indicator of how close she was to capitulating. She was only resisting him because he had rejected her advances seven years ago. He knew she had only targeted him back then because she knew it would jeopardise his relationship with her father. He'd been tempted. Sure he had. Every cell in his body had felt the strain of resisting her come-and-get-me eyes. For years he'd worked hard not to show it. Whenever he came into contact with her at one of her father's parties or events he would screen his desire behind a mask of cynicism. But inside he was simmering, smouldering with lust.

It was different now. She wanted him, not as a rebellious teenager out to make mischief. This time she wanted him as a fully grown passionate woman.

He closed down his computer and smiled. Yes. It was only a matter of time before she would be finally his.

Izzy had eaten so much she had to lie down, but she refused to lie on Andrea's bed. That seemed way too intimate, too…anticipatory, as if she was waiting for him to come and make love to her. She wasn't… But she had thought about it. A lot. It was all she seemed to think about. Her body felt agitated, restless, needy. The response he had evoked in her in the elevator had made her hungry for more. She wanted to feel his arms around her, his body within her, his mouth locked on hers.

She had a reputation as a sleep-around slut but she'd only had a handful of lovers and none of them had been satisfying. She'd always been uncomfortable with physical intimacy and had made herself tipsy in order to get through it. None of her partners had taken the time to get to know her needs or preferences but carried on regardless. She figured it was easier to pretend she was having a good time rather than speak up and risk being called a freak or frigid.

Not that she felt frigid when she was around Andrea. Far from it. He only had to put his knee between her thighs and she'd shattered into a million pieces of bliss. What would happen if he made love to her in every sense of the word?

Izzy curled up on one of the sofas in the sitting room and wrapped herself in one of the cashmere throw rugs. She had to stop thinking about Andrea making love to her. She had to stop craving his touch. She had to stop imagining his hands and lips and tongue on her flesh. *Had. To. Stop.* She turned on the television to watch one of her favourite shows but it didn't capture her interest as it normally would. She closed her eyes and promised herself she would keep an ear out for when Andrea came back in…

Andrea entered the suite and found Izzy fast asleep on one of the sofas. She was wearing one of his hotel's bathrobes but it had fallen open, revealing the slender length of her legs. Her feet were bare and her toenails were painted in an electric blue. Her hair was tied up in a ponytail but some strands had loosened and now fell about her face. Her skin was make-up free and as pure and unblemished as a cream-coloured rose, her eyelashes and eyebrows so dark in contrast she looked like a modern version of Sleeping Beauty. He had always considered her beautiful, but without the adornment of make-up and proper hair styling she looked almost ethereal, like an angel in a Renaissance painting. Serene and untouchable.

He approached the sofa but she didn't stir. He gently straightened the throw rug so it covered her legs, then he brushed back her hair, tucking it behind the shell of her ear. She smelt of the essential oils he had selected as the signature scent of his hotel chain. She gave a little murmur and burrowed her head further against the scatter cushion she was leaning on.

He felt a jab of disappointment she hadn't woken at the sound of him entering the suite. He hadn't realised how much he'd been looking forward to sparring with her. He enjoyed the way she not only locked horns with him but threatened to rip his off and stab him with them. The way she stared him down and threw insults at him like darts. He enjoyed baiting her, watching her colour rise and her eyes flash. She hated him but she wanted him, and to him that was a sexy combination.

He began to move away when she suddenly jerked upright, pushing her hair out of her face and looking at him through narrowed eyes. 'What are you doing?'

'I was covering your legs with the throw rug.'

She got up from the sofa and tied the edges of her bathrobe more securely, her cheeks stained a light pink. 'Have you eaten?' She glanced at the dinner trolley and her cheeks darkened a notch. 'I was kind of hungry so you might need to order up some more.'

Andrea picked up the bottle of champagne out of the ice bucket. 'Fancy some?'

'It might seem strange to you but I don't actually feel like celebrating.' Her tone was so sour it would have curdled milk.

He uncorked the bottle and poured two glasses. 'You should celebrate. You're now a very wealthy young woman.' He handed her a glass of champagne. 'A very wealthy *married* young woman.'

Her eyes flashed and her mouth thinned. She took the champagne and for a moment he wondered if she was going to throw it in his face. Then she touched her glass against his. 'That is if we last the distance.' She gave a small frown. 'How can I be sure you won't sabotage this by walking out before the six months is up? As you so kindly pointed out, I have the most to lose.'

Andrea stroked a finger down the curve of her cheek. 'You'll have to trust me, won't you, *cara*?'

Something hardened in her eyes and she brushed his hand away from her face as if she were shooing away a fly, almost spilling her champagne in the process. 'Stop touching me. I can't think when you do that. And I thought I told you not to keep calling me that. No one's here but us. It's totally unnecessary and it's damn annoying.'

'What you find annoying is how much you like

it when I call you that,' Andrea said. 'You like lots of the things I do to you but you're too proud to admit it.'

She plonked her glass down on the nearest surface. 'I'm going to bed.' She threw him another glare. 'And no, that is not an invitation for you to join me.'

Andrea put his glass down and came to her, taking her by the hands before she could step away. 'I will not take advantage of you, Isabella. We'll only make love if or when you give me the go-ahead. You have my absolute word on that.'

She didn't try to pull away from his hold and her expression softened slightly, the tight muscles of her jaw eased and her eyes lost their sheen of don't-mess-with-me brittleness. 'I still don't understand why you're doing this… Why you wanted to marry me in the first place. It doesn't make sense.'

He massaged the backs of her hands with his thumbs, holding her gaze with his. 'Remember I told you it was convenient for me to get married just now? I have a hotel merger I've been negotiating for a while. The owner has a teenage stepdaughter who has developed a rather embarrassing crush on me. I figured if I had a wife then that little problem will be taken care of until I get the merger completed. A temporary marriage between us seemed a perfect solution to both of our problems.'

Izzy's expression looked like she had eaten something that had disagreed with her. 'What a pity you didn't think to pull a convenient wife out of a hat seven years ago when I made that pass at you.'

'I knew what you were up to back then. You wanted to embarrass your father.' He gave her hands another slow stroke with his thumbs. 'It would have been wrong for me to get involved with you, not just because of my relationship with your father but because you were too young and headstrong to be in a proper adult relationship.'

Her teeth pulled at her lower lip, her eyes lowered. 'He always made me feel so inadequate…so stupid and useless.' Her voice held a note of bitterness that underlined each word.

Andrea frowned. Was she talking about the man he had known and admired for his business acumen and charitable work? 'Your father?'

She pulled out of his hold, her eyes glittering with the bitterness he'd heard in her voice. 'I don't want to talk about it. Not to you.'

'Why not to me?'

Her gaze shifted. 'You wouldn't believe me, that's why.'

Andrea had always been aware that there were facets to Benedict Byrne that were less honourable than others. It was why he had distanced himself from Benedict over the last couple of years. He knew Benedict had found being the father of a wilful daughter a complex and emotionally draining experience. But he realised he had only ever heard Benedict's side. He had never asked Izzy directly what it was like for her being her father's daughter. 'I'd like you to tell me, Isabella,' he said. 'It's important to me to know why you felt he didn't value you.'

Her gaze was wary. Guarded. 'Important to you, why? So you can tell me what a screwed-up, selfish and spoilt brat I am for not appreciating all the sacrifices my father made? No, thanks. I'll go and find a brick wall to talk to instead. I bet I'd feel more listened to.'

Andrea could see it was going to take some time for Izzy to learn to trust him. Their relationship had always been a combative one so changing it would take time and careful handling on his part. But it concerned him he might have been too quick to judge her in the past, too quick to believe the things her father told him about her without speaking to her himself. He'd been so intent on avoiding her, of being alone with her, he had let himself be swayed by her father's version of her behaviour.

'I'm sorry you think I wouldn't listen to you about something this important,' he said. 'Your father wasn't perfect. I had to set limits with him at times

because he could be a little overpowering in his en-
thusiasm for a project. I always felt a little sorry for
him for the loss of your brother and your mother. I
may have let that colour my judgement of him and,
of course, you.'

Izzy's expression lost some of its wariness, her
mouth softening from a tight white line of bitterness
to release a jagged sigh. 'He acted like Father of the
Year when he was around everyone else, but when
we were alone he was always berating me. Putting
me down, telling me I wasn't as smart as my brother,
Hamish, or I was too fat or too thin or not confident
enough—the list went on and on. I was never able
to please him. Never.'

Andrea knew Benedict Byrne had been a difficult man at times. He hadn't suffered fools gladly
and he had exacting standards that hadn't always
won him lasting friendships. Andrea tried to recall
all the times he'd seen Izzy and her father together.
All he could remember was Izzy acting out, being
rude or belligerent, deliberately defying curfews and
blatantly disregarding her father's wishes. Benedict
had always seemed so patient with her—far more
patient than one would expect any parent to be. Andrea had always seen Izzy as a typical overindulged
and ungrateful teenager who didn't understand the
sacrifices her father had made for her.

But what if he had misread things?

What if he had wanted to see her that way? What if *Benedict* had wanted him to see her that way?

What if the man he'd admired and owed so much was not the decent and hardworking man Benedict Byrne wanted everyone to think he was? Andrea had personal experience of chameleon-like men. His stepfather could be utterly charming in company but could turn into an anger-crazed demon when no one was looking.

'Isabella…' Andrea said, not sure where to begin with an apology that was too little, too late. 'You're describing someone I barely recognise—'

'So you'll believe what my father wanted you to believe other than accept what I'm telling you.' She didn't say it as a question but as a given, as if it was a reality she had heard many times before.

'No. I want to listen to your side. I want to understand why you found him so difficult to love.'

Her eyes suddenly brimmed with unshed tears and he realised he had never seen her cry before. Not even at her father's funeral. 'He didn't love me so why would I love him?' Her tone was defiant but underneath there was a deep chord of sadness.

He blotted one of her tears with his thumb. 'But you did love him, *si*?'

She swallowed and blinked a few times, the tears

drying up as if she regretted losing control. Her expression tightened as if all of her facial muscles were holding in her emotions and only just managing to contain them. 'You knew him as Benedict Byrne the successful business developer. As your friend and mentor. The philanthropic businessman who gave generously to others. You didn't know him as a father.'

Andrea thought again of the times he'd seen Izzy and her father together. But this time it was like putting on a different pair of reading glasses, the images developing a startling new clarity. Images of Benedict's calm expression when Izzy had made a cutting comment—he had almost been *too* calm.

Deadly calm.

Revenge-will-come-later calm.

Images of Benedict's arm around Izzy's waist and her rigid body posture, which Andrea had always put down to her surly and intractable nature. But what if Benedict's hold had a touch of cruelty about it? Benedict had spoken at length to Andrea about his hurt and disappointment over Izzy's behaviour, but what if those cosy little man-to-man confessions had been nothing but a cover-up? An emotional alibi to hide the ugly truth?

'You're right,' Andrea said. 'And no father is the same for every child within a family. I know the loss of Hamish devastated him, as it would any parent.'

'I'm not saying he didn't love my brother,' Izzy said. 'He did. But that was part of the problem. He didn't have enough love left over for me. I was just a girl and I didn't have the skills and abilities Hamish had. I was a failure in my father's eyes. A big, fat disappointing failure.'

Andrea gently placed his hands on her shoulders. 'Did he say that to you?'

Her lips pulled tight as if she wasn't sure if she should say any more. Then she let out a long breath. 'Many times. But never within anyone's hearing. My only chance to get back at him was to act out in public. I know it was stupid of me. It only made him look all the more wonderful because he was always so long-suffering and patient when anyone was watching.'

Andrea's scalp began to prickle, his stomach pinching, his conscience grimacing in shame. *He had been fooled by Benedict.* Shockingly, shamefully fooled. It was even more painful for him to admit it, given he had suffered under his stepfather's tyrannical rule, while everyone thought it was Izzy's fault for being defiant. 'What happened when everyone left?'

'He was too smart to shout at me because of the household staff who might overhear. He would tell me what he thought of me behind closed doors in this really hushed and angry voice and his eyes would get all bulgy and mad-looking.' Pain flickered over her face. 'He'd tell me how he wished I'd been the one to die instead of Hamish.'

Izzy was painting a picture Andrea didn't want to look at in too close detail but he knew he must. He couldn't allow himself to be blinded by his own personal bias. He had always prided himself on being a good judge of character but now he felt as if he had been duped. Duped by someone he had admired. He had benefited so much from her father. He would not be the success he was today without the older man's help. But he knew even the best men could have bad sides.

But how bad had Benedict Byrne's been?

'Was he ever…violent?' He stumbled over the word and all its ugliness.

'Only once.' Her eyes flashed with bitterness. 'He slapped me across the face when I was fourteen, soon after my mother died of cancer. The irony is that I told him much the same he told me. I told him I wished he'd been the one to die instead of my mother. He never hit me after that but the threat he might do so again was always there.'

Andrea was shocked and ashamed he hadn't picked up earlier on the Byrne family dynamics. He'd met her father in Italy twenty years ago, not long after the tragedy of Hamish's diagnosis of terminal bone cancer. When Benedict found Andrea begging for food on the streets, he'd been exactly the same age as the son and heir Benedict had just buried. Fourteen. There was a part of Andrea that had always wondered if Benedict would have given him the leg up he had if it hadn't been for the loss of his son. But he had been so grateful for the help he never questioned the motives behind it.

'I'm sorry you went through such treatment at the hands of someone who was supposed to love and protect you,' Andrea said. 'I only knew your father as a generous man who liked making a difference in people's lives. But I realise all people have shadow sides. But he kept his hidden far better than most.'

'So you…believe me?' The note of uncertainty in her voice made him realise what little hope she must have held that he would believe the version she had shared of her father. Had she tried to tell others and not been believed? Or hadn't she even bothered trying, knowing how hard it would be to dispel the good father image Benedict had exhibited so convincingly?

Andrea slid his hands down from her shoulders to take her hands again. 'I believe you. I thought I knew your father pretty well. But I once lived with a man who had two faces, the one he showed in public and the one he revealed in private. No one would have believed him capable of the things he did in private. I'm sorry I didn't cotton on to Benedict earlier. I would have spoken to him. Called him out on his behaviour.'

She looked down at their joined hands, releasing a little shuddery breath. Then her gaze climbed back to his. 'He was awful to Mum as well. She had no hope of standing up to him. She'd bought into the belief that wives should always obey their husbands. She took all his insults and put-downs, which made me so angry and all the more determined to stand up to him to show him he couldn't push me around the same way. But I'm not sure it worked the way I intended. I ended up wrecking my own life...'

Andrea could see why Izzy had railed against his insistence they marry. He'd hardly given her a choice. He'd acted like an overbearing army sergeant issuing commands and orders. No wonder she'd pushed back and fought him at every opportunity. 'Isabella...I don't know what to say, other than I'm sorry things have turned out like this. Your father had no right to treat you and your mother like that. I'm shocked and deeply ashamed I didn't suspect it earlier. I guess the only consolation is he's left you well provided for, even if the conditions attached to his will are not what you would have chosen.'

Her expression became brooding and resentful. 'But that's the point—he didn't expect me to fulfil the conditions of his will. He knew how much I hated the thought of marriage, of giving up my freedom. He made his feelings for me perfectly clear. He would rather give all of his wealth—a large proportion of which originally belonged to my mother—to a distant relative with a gambling problem than give it outright to me, his only remaining heir.'

Andrea could see so clearly now there were things about Izzy's father he had ignored the whole time he'd known him. Ignored or dismissed or excused. Why hadn't he taken the time to look a little more closely? He'd made allowances for Izzy's father because he felt sorry for all Benedict had suffered in losing a son and having to deal with a difficult daughter and a grief-stricken wife, and then the subsequent loss of his wife to liver cancer. Andrea had been too ready to lay the blame at Izzy's door, believing her to be the problem. He'd taken the view that Benedict was doing all he could to keep what was left of his family together, throwing himself into work and charitable causes to compensate for his terrible loss. Izzy's mother had struggled both physically and mentally since Hamish's death, as any mother would, but Benedict had always given Andrea the impression he was a loving husband and father, endlessly, tirelessly patient and hardworking.

Andrea felt sick to his gut he hadn't realised the truth earlier. Shame ran through his body like a fetid tide. He'd married Izzy with the intention of 'taming' her. He'd been intent on schooling her like a flighty filly, but how crass and boorish that seemed now.

It made one thing clear to him, though. How could he consummate the marriage now he knew the history of her relationship with her father? How could he cross that boundary, knowing what he knew now? But it wasn't the physical boundary he was most worried about. Getting close to her would mean crossing an emotional boundary he never crossed with anyone. Although it would just about kill him to keep his hands off her he would do the right thing by her—see the six months out so she received her inheritance— but it would be a paper marriage.

He let out a long breath. 'I wasn't comfortable with the way your father wrote his will, but I didn't consider it my place to interfere with his wishes.'

A frown pulled at her smooth brow. 'Why weren't you comfortable?'

'I was concerned you might marry someone in haste who would do the wrong thing by you.'

'So you volunteered your…erm, services?'

Andrea released her and put a little distance between them. He had to get himself out of the habit of touching her. *Hands off. Hands off. Hands off.* It was a mantra inside his head but the rest of his body wasn't listening.

If he were truly honest with himself, he wasn't exactly sure why he'd stepped into the breach and offered to marry her. *Forced, not offered.* He cringed at how he'd made it virtually impossible for her to refuse. But a part of his reasoning had been that he hadn't liked the thought of her marrying some creep who would take half her inheritance in a subsequent divorce. He hadn't liked the thought of her marrying anyone…other than him. 'Here's the thing. I'd been rethinking our paper marriage deal, offering you a six-month affair that would suit both our ends. But, knowing what I know now, well, that's not going to happen.'

Shock flashed over her features. 'You're not thinking of walking out on our—?'

'No. Of course not.' He gave her a reassuring smile. 'We will stay in the marriage for six months, as the will states, but, as agreed, it will be a marriage in name only.'

CHAPTER SIX

IN NAME ONLY... Izzy was shocked at how disappointed she felt at those three little words. A crushing, stomach-hollowing disappointment. She should be feeling relieved...but ever since that interlude in the elevator, privately all she had wanted was to have Andrea make love to her.

Properly. Naked. Skin to skin.

But in the midst of her shock and disappointment was relief that he had listened to her and believed her about her father's behaviour. She'd expected him to shut her down or to say there was no way her father could have been so unkind.

But he hadn't.

He'd listened and soothed and comforted her when her emotions had threatened to overspill. It softened some—*not all*—of the antagonism she felt towards Andrea. He was still her arch-enemy; she had seen him as such for too long for that to change in a hurry. But that didn't mean they couldn't make the most of the time they had together, did it?

But now he was refusing to consummate their marriage. What was she supposed to feel about that? Why wasn't she happy? She should be happy. She should be ecstatic. She would get her inheritance and her freedom when the six months was up.

But she wouldn't get Andrea.

She wouldn't experience the passion and fire of his lovemaking, the searing possession of his kisses and caresses. She would never know what it was like to spend the night in his arms. Never know what it was like to feel his body move within hers. Never know what her body was capable of when being pleasured by his.

Izzy drew the edges of her bathrobe around her body, unsure of what to do with her hands. She wanted to reach for him. To tell him not to be so silly, not to be so damn honourable. To beg him to make love to her. But she had already shown too much vulnerability this evening, far more than she'd ever shown to anyone. 'It sounds like you've given this some thought...' She couldn't remove the note of disappointment from her voice.

'I have and I believe it's the best way forward. The *only* way forward.' His tone had an edge of finality that precluded further discussion on the topic.

Izzy picked up her abandoned champagne glass and took a sip. 'If I'd told you earlier about my father would you still have married me?'

Andrea took his glass as if he too needed something to do with his hands. He swirled the contents for a moment, watching as the bubbles danced in a little whirlpool. 'I considered offering three months ago but decided it was better to wait.'

'Until I was desperate.' Izzy didn't ask it as a question, more as a wry statement of fact.

He gave a brief smile. 'I can't imagine what is wrong with all the young men in London. You should have been snatched up years ago.'

Izzy made a grimace. 'Don't you read the gossip pages? I'm not exactly ideal wife material. I'm the girl men have flings with before they settle down with someone far more suitable.'

Something flickered over his face. 'Women are entitled to have just as many sexual encounters as men if that's what they want to do.'

Izzy frowned. 'So you're not judging me for my past? Is that what you're saying?'

His gaze became direct, like a detective examining important evidence. 'How much of your past is fact and how much is fiction?'

She gave an offhand shrug to cover how exposed she suddenly felt. Why had she got herself into this conversation? She wasn't interested in getting his good opinion... Well, maybe that wasn't quite true. There was a part of her that did want his approval. She wanted it far more than she should. 'Make a guess.'

'If what they write about me is any indication, I would say not much is true.' He kept his gaze trained on hers. 'Am I correct?'

Izzy toyed with her champagne glass. 'In the early days I would deliberately court negative attention from the press. I wanted to embarrass my father and I didn't care how I achieved it. Pictures of me stumbling out of nightclubs in the early hours of the morning were my modus operandi. It was so easy. All I had to do was look a little wasted and they would take the money shot. I soon got a reputation for wild partying but the truth was much more boring.'

His expression was shadowed with a combination of confusion and concern. 'Were you drunk at your father's Christmas party when you were eighteen or just pretending?'

Izzy gave a regretful sigh. 'Not drunk, tipsy—just as I was every year. It was the only way I could get through my father's Devoted Dad act. Silly, now that I think about it. The only person I ended up hurting was myself.'

Andrea touched her on the arm. 'Reputations can

be repaired in time. But it's important *you* feel good about yourself. What other people think isn't something you can control.'

Did she feel good about herself? Izzy wasn't sure she could answer that with any certainty. A childhood of being told she wasn't good enough wasn't an easy thing to dismiss. She felt those negatives messages in the fabric of her soul. They were like bruises that would throb whenever self-doubt bumped against them. She forced a smile. 'I think I'll have to work on that.'

He lifted her chin with his finger, his eyes holding hers for a long, intense moment. His gaze flicked to her mouth and his throat tightened over a swallow. His hand fell away from her face and he stepped back. 'You have the bed. I'll take the sofa.'

Izzy could still feel the tingle from his touch and the ache of disappointment that he hadn't kissed her. The air seemed charged with energy—a sexual energy that made her skin prickle and tighten. 'Andrea?' Her voice came out soft and husky.

The muscles of his face tensed as if he was garnering his resolve. 'We need to be sensible about this, Isabella.' The stern drill sergeant note was back in his voice as if he were speaking to an insubordinate refusing an exercise.

'What is sensible about a six-foot-four man trying

to sleep on a sofa?' Izzy said. 'We can share the bed without touching, surely? It's certainly big enough.'

'Believe me. It's not big enough.' His tone was dry.

Izzy frowned. 'But what about the housekeeping staff? Didn't you say you wanted everyone to think our marriage was genuine?'

He let out a slowly rationed breath. 'We will fly to Positano tomorrow. There's more privacy at my villa as I keep staff down to a minimum. My housekeeper is the soul of discretion. You can have your own room and she won't say a word.'

'But what about my job? And my studies? I have to call my boss and—'

'I've already seen to it,' Andrea said. 'He wishes you well. And you can study anywhere these days as long as you've got access to Wi-Fi.'

'You've thought of everything.' Izzy hadn't meant to sound so cynical but everything was spinning out of her control. Had been from the moment she'd accepted his offer of marriage. She wasn't used to it. But another part of her—a secret part—was enjoying having someone take care of her.

Andrea turned away and poured himself a small measure of the champagne they'd had earlier. She suspected it had more to do with him needing to do something with his hands than any desire for more alcohol. She had never seen him drink to excess. It was another thing she had, albeit reluctantly, admired about him. 'Go to bed, Isabella.'

'Why do you always call me by my full name instead of Izzy?'

He took a sip of his drink and then lowered the glass to look at her, his thumb moving on the side of the glass in a circular motion. 'It's a beautiful name. Elegant and regal. Sophisticated.'

Izzy gave a little snort. 'I'm hardly what anyone would describe as sophisticated.'

'You're too hard on yourself.' His voice had a softer note that glided along her skin like a caress.

Izzy forced a smile. 'I'll leave you to it, then. I'm feeling pretty tired. It's been a big day.'

She was almost at the door of the bedroom when his voice stalled her. 'Were you disappointed we didn't have a more formal church wedding?'

Izzy turned to look at him but there was nothing in his expression she could read, other than mild interest. 'I never intended getting married in a church or otherwise so how could I be disappointed?'

He gave a slight nod as if her answer made perfect sense, but there was a shadow in the back of his gaze that made her wonder if he would ever take what she said at face value again. It unnerved her to think she had revealed so much to him in so short a time. Impersonal or not, their wedding ceremony had shifted something in their relationship. It was not the same as before. She was finding it harder and harder to see him as the enemy, especially when his touch made her feel so alive. She needed to keep him at a distance—an emotional distance—if she were to get out of this six-month marriage without getting hurt.

Izzy somehow managed to sleep in spite of her worries about the new shape of her relationship with Andrea. But it appeared the same couldn't be said of him when she came out of the suite the next morning. He looked like he'd been awake all night. Dark stubble peppered his jaw and his eyes were drawn and his hair looked like it had suffered the repeated shove of his fingers. He unfolded himself from the sofa and rubbed the back of his neck. 'How did you sleep?' he asked, wincing against the sunlight when she drew back the curtains.

'Clearly a whole lot better than you,' Izzy said, picking up the throw rug that had fallen to the floor and folding it neatly into a square. She hugged it against her body. 'Shall I make you some coffee?'

'You don't have to wait on me, Isabella.' The gruff note in his voice nicked at her fraught nerves.

She placed the throw rug over the end of the sofa

and straightened. 'Are you usually this grumpy in the mornings?'

'Grumpier.'

She raised her brows. 'Even after a night of hot sex?' *You should not have asked that.*

Something darkened in his gaze. 'There's not usually someone around in the morning to witness my mood.'

Izzy frowned. 'You mean you don't allow sleep-overs?'

'No.' There was an emphatic tone to the word that made her wonder what made him insist on such a rule.

'Is that in the playboy's rulebook? No emotional entanglements, no cosy pillow talk?'

His mouth moved in a wry smile that didn't quite reach his eyes. 'I don't like giving mixed signals. Sex is sex. It's not a promise of forever.'

'But what if you see the same person for a few weeks or even months? You've had such relationships, surely?'

'Occasionally.'

'And?'

'I don't like morning-after-the-night-before scenes,' he said. 'It's much simpler to make sure they don't happen in the first place. Then no expectations get raised. No one gets hurt.'

Izzy studied him for a moment. 'It kind of makes me wonder what sort of women you've dated. I wouldn't be too keen on a man who didn't want to see me wake up beside him the next morning. I'd find it insulting if he asked me to leave once the deed was done.'

'I make sure they're more than adequately compensated.'

'What with? Flowers, chocolates or designer jewellery delivered to their door the next day?'

'No jewellery.'

'Why?'

'It's too…personal.'

Izzy moved across to the tea and coffee making area in the suite, busying herself with the task of making herself a cup of tea. She didn't want to think about the women he'd dated. Or the fact that he'd bought her a gorgeous diamond and sapphire ring and wedding ring. *What did that mean?* But the voice of reason came down hard on her silly romantic musing. It meant he wanted everyone to think this was a real marriage and not a six months sham. She turned to glance at him over her shoulder. 'Are you sure about that cup of coffee?'

'Quite sure.'

Izzy reached for a luxury muslin teabag and dropped it into her cup. 'I guess I should congratulate myself on being the first woman you've bought jewellery for.' She turned and looked at him again. 'Or do you want me to give the rings back when we annul this marriage?'

His eyes went to her mouth, lingering there for a heart-stopping moment as if wondering if their marriage was ever going to stay unconsummated. His gaze returned to hers but a screen had come up. 'They're nothing but props. You can keep them or give them away or sell them. It doesn't matter to me.' He turned and strode to the suite she had not long vacated.

After a few minutes she heard the shower running and she sat and quietly sipped her tea, trying not to picture him naked under that hot stream of water where she had showered not half an hour ago.

Andrea stood under the punishing spray of the shower, trying to wash away his unruly desire. He'd made a promise to keep their marriage unconsummated but every time he was within touching distance of Izzy his body went on high alert. Every cell in his body wanted her. He ached with the need to hold her, to feel her body pressed against his, to feel her response to him. A response he knew would be as passionate and heady as her kiss had been. Knowing what he did now about her father made him even more determined to keep his promise. But Izzy seemed determined to poke at his resolve to see if it was as firm as he claimed.

He closed his eyes under the shower spray but he could still picture her mouth. Could still feel it moving beneath his. How many times had he wanted to forget about his damn principles and stride into that bedroom last night and join her in that bed? Desire had throbbed in him all night in fierce combat with his resolve to resist the temptation. It had made it impossible for him to sleep. All he could think about was Izzy lying on his sheets next door, her hair splayed out over his pillow, her slim sexy limbs stretched out and her gorgeous breasts on show. The breasts he fantasised about touching, caressing, kissing until she whimpered with the same longing he could feel thrumming in his blood.

How would he survive six months of this torture?

He would go mad in the process. He wondered now if it was a mistake to whisk her with him to Italy, but the London paparazzi were unbearable. At his private villa in Positano he could at least keep such intrusions to a minimum. And his long-term housekeeper, Gianna, was the soul of discretion. Gianna was the only person he would trust with the secret of his marriage to Izzy.

No one else must know it wasn't the real deal.

Andrea stepped out of the shower and roughly dried himself, trying not to think of how Izzy had stood in this very spot earlier. Her used towel was hung neatly back on the rail, her cosmetics tidily put back into her toiletries bag. There was a trace of her flowery perfume lingering in the air.

When he came out of the bathroom with a towel slung around his hips, Izzy was sitting on the end of the king-sized bed scrolling through her phone. She looked up and her eyes darted to the towel and then back to his gaze. She sprang up from the bed, her cheeks staining a soft pink. 'I'll leave you to get dressed.'

Andrea shouldn't have reached for her. His mind said, *Don't do it*, but his body had other ideas. Wicked, forbidden ideas over which he had no control. His fingers encircled her slim wrist and he felt the flutter of her pulse under the pad of his thumb. 'Don't run away.' His voice was so husky it sounded like he'd swallowed a handful of gravel.

Her eyes rounded and her throat moved up and down over a swallow. 'I thought you said we were going to be sensible about this…?'

Andrea lifted her hand to his face, pressing a kiss to her bent knuckles. 'I said no sleeping together. But I didn't say no touching. We'll be expected to touch in public. It would look strange if we didn't.' Even he could hear how he was rationalising his behaviour, but he didn't much care. He felt like he would die if he didn't touch her.

Doubt flickered in her gaze. 'What sort of touching?'

He slid his hand along the side of her face until his fingers were enmeshed in her fragrant hair, the silky strands tickling his fingers. Her eyes shone with anticipation, the same anticipation he could feel rolling through his body with unstoppable force.

'This,' he said, bringing his mouth to within a breath of hers. He didn't touch down, but nudged her soft lips with his, once, twice, three times.

Her lips quivered as if she was fighting her own battle to resist the temptation he had laid before her. Her breath mingled with his, sweet and fresh with a hint of vanilla. Her tongue crept out and left a layer of moisture on her lips. He moved that little bit closer to her, his thighs coming into contact with hers. He could feel the quake of awareness that shot through her like aftershocks. Her breasts bumped into his chest. He placed a hand at the small of her back and pressed her closer, his body erupting into flames when he felt her softness against his hardness. He was intoxicated with her closeness. The smell of her. Her womanly heat igniting him like a match to tinder.

His mouth covered hers and he swallowed her sigh of pleasure. Her arms came up to link around his neck, her body pressed so tightly against him he could feel every soft pliable contour. Her mouth opened under his, her tongue tangling with his in a sexy duel that made his blood head south in a throbbing gush. He took control of the kiss, holding her face in his hands to get better access, his tongue stabbing and flicking against hers in a mimic of what his body wanted more than anything. He finally lifted his mouth off hers, resting his forehead against hers as he fought for control. 'Maybe this wasn't such a great idea.'

Izzy's hands began to toy with his hair, sending hot darting tingles down his spine and deeper into his groin. 'It's just a kiss...' Her eyes met his. 'Isn't it?'

Andrea wasn't sure if he had the self-control to just kiss her. What had he been thinking? He was pushing himself beyond his limits. Torturing himself with what he wanted but couldn't—*shouldn't*—have. He traced her mouth with a lazy finger, watching as she quivered again against his touch. 'You have such a beautiful mouth.' He couldn't seem to keep the gravel out of his tone.

Her eyes went to his mouth, the tip of her tongue sneaking out to moisten her lips once more. 'Yours isn't so bad either.' She brought one of her hands down from around his neck to trace over his bottom lip. 'It's a lot softer than it looks.'

He captured her hand and pressed a kiss to the tip of her finger, holding her gaze with his. 'There isn't a whole lot of me that's soft right now.'

Her cheeks were delicately tinged with pink. 'So I can feel.' She moved against him, a subtle shift that sent an earthquake of lust through his body. His self-control strained at the leash like a rabid dog. Blood pounded and pulsed through his veins, driven by raw primal need. Had he ever wanted someone as much as he wanted her? Or was it because he had made a promise to himself not to have her? There was a war inside him. A raging battle he wasn't sure he could win.

But he would have to win it.

He couldn't allow things to get any more complicated than they already were. But a kiss or two was fine. That wasn't going to do any harm…was it?

He gripped her by the hips, holding her to him, not caring how much it was torturing him. He wanted. Wanted. Wanted her with a need so great it blasted every other thought out of his head. He brought his mouth back down to hers, crushing her to him, his tongue tangling with the moist heat of hers. He slid his hands down the sides of her body and then up again, slipping underneath her top and travelling up her smooth skin, stopping just below the satin curve of her breasts. He stepped back from her with a willpower he hadn't known he possessed, his body thrumming, humming, aching with need.

Disappointment flared in her eyes. But then her expression became masked and she stepped away from him and straightened her clothes. 'What time is our flight?'

Andrea tried not to look at her kiss-swollen mouth and the little patch of stubble rash on her chin. Seeing that intimate marking on her soft creamy skin made something in his stomach slip sideways. He tightened the towel around his hips and moved across to the wardrobe to dress. 'We leave at eleven a.m. Your things will be sent on from your flat. If you need anything else we can buy it in Italy.' He closed the wardrobe and turned back around but she had gone.

CHAPTER SEVEN

A FEW HOURS later they arrived via chauffeur-driven car at Andrea's private villa high on the slopes above the seaside village of Positano. Izzy hadn't been to the Amalfi coast for years and yet it was as magical and picturesque as she remembered it. The startling blue of the ocean below, the wincingly bright sunshine from a perfectly clear sky and the scent of fragrant blossom from the luxurious garden at the villa made her senses sing with joy. Scarlet bougainvillea cascaded from a stone wall, standing pots and hanging baskets of red and white geraniums provided more eye-popping colour. Birds twittered in the shrubs and hedges behind, and in front of the villa was an infinity pool that overlooked the view of the coast below. It was picture postcard perfect and Izzy couldn't imagine a nicer place to hide away from the penetrating eyes of the public and the press.

Andrea led her to the front door of the villa but,

before he could unlock it, an older woman dressed all in black opened it. Her sun-weathered face was wreathed in smiles and her black button eyes twinkled like the sun-dappled ocean below. A torrent of Italian came pouring out of her mouth but Izzy could only understand a couple of words, which she took to be an enthusiastic welcome. Such a welcome seemed a little surprising given the circumstances of her marriage to Andrea, but then she didn't know what he'd told his housekeeper.

'English please, Gianna,' Andrea said.

The housekeeper beamed brighter than a searchlight. '*Mi dispiace*. Sorry. I am so excited to welcome Signor's new bride to Villa Vaccaro. You have had a good journey, *sì*?'

'Lovely, thank you,' Izzy said, warming to the older woman's friendly nature.

'I have prepared the master bedroom for you,' Gianna said, sweeping her hand in front of the entrance. 'You must carry your bride over the threshold, *sì*?'

Andrea frowned. 'Gianna. I thought I'd told you not to make a fuss. Isabella requires her own room.'

Gianna rolled her eyes like marbles. 'You bring a beautiful bride home and you expect me to make up the spare room for her? Pah! What sort of marriage is that?'

'A marriage of convenience sort, that's what.'

Andrea's voice had a thread of impatience running through it. 'Isabella and I don't intend for this arrangement to last longer than the six months required to fulfil the terms of her father's will. I explained all this when I called you last night.'

The housekeeper was clearly not intimidated by her employer's stern expression. She stood her ground with her arms folded and her dark gaze fixed on Andrea's frowning one. 'Marriage of convenience or not, you should still carry her over the threshold. It's bad luck not to.'

Andrea let out an exasperated breath and turned to Izzy. 'Do you mind?'

'Not at all,' Izzy said, trying not to laugh. She wasn't used to seeing Andrea backed into a tight corner. It showed a softer side to him she hadn't seen before. He clearly cared for and respected his housekeeper and was prepared to indulge her even if it was inconvenient to him.

Andrea scooped Izzy up in his strong arms and she linked her arms around his neck. The iron bands of his arm along her back and beneath her knees sent her senses spinning. His jaw was set in a tight line and his mouth pressed flat, but even so she could feel the way his body responded to her closeness. The way his nostrils flared as if he were taking in her scent, the way his hooded gaze went to her mouth.

The contraction of his abdomen muscles where her body brushed against him. She couldn't help wondering what it would be like if she really was his bride of choice. What if their on-paper arrangement was torn up and they gave in to the passion and heat that simmered and smouldered and sizzled between them? How wonderful it would be for him to whisk her upstairs to the master suite and make earth-rocking love to her.

He set her down in front of him inside the villa but he kept hold of one of her hands. 'You'll have to excuse my housekeeper,' he said once Gianna was out of earshot. 'She's a hopeless romantic.'

'I like her,' Izzy said. 'How long has she worked for you?'

'Clearly too long since she's ignoring my instructions.' His tone had a dry edge. 'I'll get her to show you around. I have some things to see to in my office. Gianna?' he called out to the housekeeper, who had moved further inside the villa. 'Please show Isabella to the guest room.'

Izzy followed Gianna up the sweeping staircase, wondering if Andrea had pressing business to see to or whether he was putting distance between them because of the reaction of his housekeeper to his marriage.

Gianna led the way to a lovely suite on the first

floor of the four-storey villa with a breathtaking view over the coast. 'Signor Vaccaro's suite is next door. See? There is a connecting door here.' She pointed out the door with a twinkling smile. 'Not that I think you'll need the key, *si*? I see the way he looks at you.'

Izzy could feel a blush stealing over her cheeks. 'It really is a marriage of convenience. Neither of us really want to be married and certainly not to each other.' Hadn't the housekeeper heard about Izzy's reputation? It seemed a little odd Gianna was so enthusiastic about their union given all that had been reported about Izzy in the past.

Gianna made another one of her *'pah'* noises and started fussing over the pillows on the bed. 'He has known you for a long time, *si*?'

'Yes, but we're hardly what you'd call best friends.'

Gianna straightened and turned to look at her. 'Your father was very good to him. He helped him get started in the hotel business. He is not a man to forget those who have helped him.'

'Did you ever meet my father?'

Gianna turned to a vase of fresh flowers on the table near the window but not before Izzy saw her expression sour slightly. 'He was a guest here once or twice. He was keen to tell me about all the charity causes he supports.' Gianna picked up a fallen pale pink rose petal and popped it in her apron pocket. She turned and looked at Izzy again. 'I was sorry to hear of his passing for the sake of those charities if nothing else. I'm sorry. I'm speaking out of turn. You must miss him, *si*?'

Izzy gave a lip shrug. 'Yes and no.'

Gianna's gaze narrowed in query. 'You were not close?'

'Not particularly.'

The housekeeper shifted her lips from side to side in a musing manner. 'Yes, well, I wondered about that when Andrea told me about your father's will. It was a strange thing to do to his only heir, was it not?'

'Not strange if you knew my father,' Izzy said with a sigh. 'We had a complicated relationship.'

Gianna tut-tutted. 'But all is well now you are married to Andrea. He will take good care of you. He will make sure you get your inheritance. He is an honourable man, not that he boasts about all the good he does for others. No one would ever know about the many charities he supports. He insists on anonymity. I only know because I dust his office and came across the paperwork. You are a little bit in love with him, *si*?'

Izzy didn't like to burst the housekeeper's romantic bubble but her feelings towards Andrea were complex enough to her, never mind explaining them to someone else, especially to someone she'd only just met. 'Let's say I'm starting to see him in a different light.'

Gianna smiled. 'I will leave you to settle in. Would you like tea or coffee, a cool drink?'

'Tea would be lovely, but I'll come downstairs. You don't have to wait on me.'

'It is no trouble,' Gianna said. 'After all, you are the first woman Andrea has brought here to stay. That must count for something, no?'

The first woman he'd brought here to stay... It was hard not to feel a twinge of delight to think Andrea's private sanctuary had never been shared with one of his casual lovers. Why did he keep himself so separate from others? Surely it was a little unusual to spend so much time alone? No wonder the housekeeper was in such raptures about Izzy's arrival as his 'bride'. But it didn't mean he cared about her. Yes, he was honourable and had stepped up to help her claim her inheritance by marrying her according to the terms of her father's will. And he had made a promise to keep their marriage on paper so there would be a less complicated cessation of it when the time was up.

Why then was Izzy wondering if their marriage

could be more than that? Had the housekeeper's romantic fantasy nonsense brushed off on her?

She looked at the adjoining door and suppressed a shiver. She moved across the room and touched the brass key sticking out of the lock. Her fingers curled around it and she gave it a single turn but, instead of locking the door, it unlocked with an audible click.

She held her breath for a moment and watched her hand going to the doorknob as if it belonged to someone else. She turned the doorknob and the door opened into a large suite that overlooked the coast below as well as a sweep of the wooded hills and rocky outcrops on the other side. The suite smelt faintly masculine—the hint of warm citrus and cool cedar she couldn't help associating with Andrea. The décor was cream and white with black and gold trimmings that gave the room a regal air.

Izzy's eyes strayed to the king-sized bed and her head swam with images of his tanned naked body lying against the pristine white of the sheets. She went over to the bed and trailed her fingers across the nearest pillow. No one else had shared this bed with him. No one. What did that mean? That he valued his privacy. That he came here to get away from the prying eyes of the press. It didn't mean that Izzy held any special significance in his life. She was a temporary wife to solve his problem as well as her own.

The main door of the master suite opened and Andrea came in. He closed the door behind him, his eyes locking on hers with dark lustrous intensity. 'I hope you're not letting Gianna's happy-ever-after fantasy mess with your head.'

It wasn't just her head that was getting messed with—her whole body was full of restless longing. 'I was just checking the lock.' Izzy waved her hand back towards the connecting door.

'I told Gianna to put you in a suite further down the corridor.'

'Was that for my benefit or yours?'

His eyes darkened to black ink. 'Both.'

Izzy's tummy tingled at the thought of him trying to keep his distance. It was thrilling to think he was as tempted as she was to put aside their on-paper marriage and indulge in a red-hot affair. 'Gianna told me I'm the first woman you've ever brought here to stay.'

He gave a rough-sounding laugh. 'It would look odd if I didn't bring you here since we're married, would it not?'

'I think Gianna thinks you're secretly in love with me and me with you.'

His gaze became even more direct. 'And are you?'

It was Izzy's turn to laugh but she didn't quite pull it off with the same convincing ease. 'Of course not.'

He gave a stiff on-off smile. 'Better keep it that way.'

Izzy tossed her hair back behind her shoulders. 'Don't worry. I have no intention of falling in love with you.'

'But you want me.' His gaze went to her mouth and back to her eyes in a heartbeat. 'Don't you, *cara*?'

Izzy swallowed, her heart kicking up its pace the longer he held her gaze with the searing probe of his. Desire throbbed in the air like an electrical current. She felt it zinging along her flesh, up and down her spine, pooling in a cave of molten heat between her thighs. 'We agreed this was going to be a hands-off arrangement.' Why had her voice betrayed her by coming out so breathy and husky?

Andrea came to stand in front of her—every pore of her body was acutely, desperately aware of him. His eyes dipped to her mouth and a wave of longing swept through her at the thought of his hard possessive mouth taking hers captive. His hand came up and cradled the side of her face. It was such a tender caress, a disarming resolve-melting touch that made her desire for him escalate even further. His thumb moved across her cheek in a slow-moving stroke that made her skin tingle and her heart skip a beat. 'You shouldn't have come in here.' His voice was a deep bass with a grace note of gravel.

Izzy licked her suddenly bone-dry lips, her gaze

flicking to the lazy curve of his mouth. 'You should have locked and bolted the door on your side.'

He inched up her chin, meshing his gaze with hers in a sensually charged lock that made her stomach swoop. 'I'm trying to do the right thing by you, but you keep making it so damn difficult.' His thumb brushed over her lower lip, sending hot little pulses of delight through her sensitive skin. 'A sexual relationship between us will only complicate things.'

Izzy sent her tongue over where his thumb had just been and tasted his saltiness on her lip. 'I'm not asking you to sleep with me.'

A glint of cynicism lit his eyes. 'Are you not?'

She lowered her gaze from the probe of his, but looking at his mouth made her desire for him all the more intense. 'I'm not sure what I'm asking…' It was a lie. She knew exactly what she was asking. What she wanted. What she craved. Him.

He brought up her chin and meshed his gaze with hers. 'If we slept together it would only be for the duration of our marriage. You do understand that, don't you?'

Izzy placed her hands on the hard flat plane of his chest, her fingers curling into the fabric of his shirt. 'It's not like we can sleep with anyone else while we're married. So why not make the most of being tied together for six months?' She could barely believe she had been so brazen about her desire to sleep with him when for all this time she had vehemently denied wanting him. But it seemed pointless to deny it when he only had to look at her to see how much he affected her. Hadn't he always?

Andrea framed her face in his broad hands, his thumbs moving back and forth across her cheeks in a mesmerising caress that made her skin sing with delight. 'Something about this feels wrong and yet so damn right.' He brought his mouth down to hers and brushed his lips against hers. It was a soft experimental touchdown but, as if the warmth from her lips ignited a flare in his, the kiss became suddenly passionate, a bruising press of hungry lips fuelled by primitive carnal need.

Izzy was swept away by the thrilling heart-stopping force of it, the glide and thrust of his tongue against hers making her legs feel like the ligaments had been severed. It was all she could do to stay upright. Her lips clung to his, her tongue dancing and darting in intimate play, the erotic sensations travelling from her mouth to her core as if her entire network of nerves were on fire. Her heart raced with the sheer excitement of arousal. An arousal she had never felt like this before. Her whole body was tuned in to his every movement, every touch, every stroke or glide or pressure of his flesh against hers. His lips were firm and then achingly, disarmingly soft. His tongue spine-tinglingly bold and commanding. His hands moved from her face to hold her by the hips, his fingers firm and possessive and yet respectful. She didn't feel rushed or pushed or shoved. She didn't feel that this was all about him and less about her. This was a mutual exploration of need, a discovery tour of their chemistry—the chemistry that had snapped and crackled between them for years.

He brought her closer to his body, hip-to-hip, arousal-to-arousal. The hard ridge of his erection making her inner core contract, the band of his chest against her breasts making her feel more feminine than she had ever felt before. Their bodies seemed to fit together like a complicated puzzle, no awkward pieces or edges left over.

Izzy slid her hands up from his chest to tangle her fingers in his hair, tugging and releasing the thick dark strands, her mouth still fused to the magical pressure of his. His hands moved from her hips to skate up the sides of her body to settle just below her breasts. To feel them there, so close and yet not touching where she longed to be touched, was an exquisite torture. She made a whimpering sound and he moved his right hand to gently cup her breast, his thumb moving over the pointed tip of her nipple that, even through her clothes, made her snatch in a sharp breath of delight. His other hand slipped beneath her top and glided along her bare skin, the graze of his masculine fingers making her stomach free-fall. He unhooked her bra and took her breasts into his hands, cradling them, caressing them, worshipping them. He bent his head to her right breast, his tongue sending a slow lick across the upper curve before encircling her areola, leaving the nub of her nipple until last. The moist lave of his tongue made the hairs on her scalp stand up and stretch and twirl like thousands of tiny music box ballerinas. She was breathless with desire, the excitement building like a tumultuous storm inside her body.

Andrea moved to her other breast, exploring it in the same intimate detail, leaving her senses spinning with every stroke and lick of his tongue and every nudge and nibble and suckle of his lips.

Every time he caressed her another stitch came undone in her chest—the tight stitches she'd placed around her carefully guarded heart.

He led her to the bed, bringing her down with him, his mouth coming back to hers in a long drugging kiss that made her wonder why she had resisted him for so long. How could she have denied herself this magic? The thrill of his touch. The excitement of being in his arms. The dizzying pleasure she could feel building in her body, triggered by him and only him.

Andrea pushed back her hair from her face to look down into her eyes. 'Still sure about this?'

Izzy touched the stubble along his jaw, her fingers catching like silk on sandpaper. 'I'm sure.'

He planted another soft kiss to her lips, then moved his mouth in a hot trail of fire down her neck and to her décolletage. His tongue traced over each curve of her breasts, his mouth closing over each nipple in turn in a gentle suckle that made her back arch off the bed. He moved his hand down the flank of her thigh, peeling away her clothes to leave smouldering kisses in their wake. Every movement of his was slow and languorous, not rushed and threatening in any way.

Izzy worked on his shirt buttons, uncovering the muscled planes of his chest and trailing her fingers through the dusting of hair sprinkled across his chest and abdomen, arrowing down to a V to disappear below the waistband of his trousers. He drew in a breath when her fingers brushed against his taut lower abdomen and, with a boldness she would not have thought possible even hours ago, she brushed her fingers over the tented fabric of his trousers.

His dark eyes locked on hers and her belly quivered at the blatant desire gleaming there. 'I want you.

Damn it, but I want you.' His tone was gruff with a side note of resentment.

Izzy coiled her finger around a lock of his hair. 'You make it sound like it's some sort of affliction.'

He pressed a firm kiss to her mouth. 'It is. It's plagued me for years.'

She pushed his head back up by placing her hand against his forehead. 'How many years?'

He gave a lopsided smile that made something in her chest ping. 'Seven.'

Izzy outlined his mouth with her fingertip. 'So you really did want me back then.'

'Madly.' He captured her finger and closed his mouth over it, drawing on it like he had done on her nipple earlier. It was the most erotic feeling to have his tongue flickering against her finger, and her inner core reacted in anticipation.

'You told me to go away and grow up.'

'Which you have done.' His eyes glinted as they glanced at her naked breasts. 'It's been all I could do to keep my hands off you.'

Izzy took his hands and placed them on her breasts. 'I want your hands on me. I want you inside me.'

Something flickered across his gaze. 'Are you on the Pill?'

'Yes.'

'Good, because having sex is one thing, having a baby is another.'

'I'm not going to get pregnant, Andrea.' Izzy hadn't intended to snap at him but the way he was carrying on made her feel he suspected her of trying to trap him with a surprise pregnancy.

'It can happen even when precautions are taken.'

'It hasn't happened so far.'

'But if it did, what would you do?' he asked.

Izzy had never thought of having a baby. It was something other people did—they got married to someone they fancied themselves in love with and then had a child or two together. She had taught herself *not* to want such things. Watching the way her mother had suffered under the over-controlling behaviour of her father had made her wary of allowing any man to have such a hold over her. And even though she had only been five when her brother, Hamish, had died, watching the overwhelming grief her parents had gone through, particularly her mother, had further entrenched her decision to stay single and childless. Falling in love with someone would make her too vulnerable and needy. Having a child with them would only increase that vulnerability. It had always seemed far more sensible, not to mention safer, to keep men at an emotional distance.

Thinking about a baby and Andrea in the same

sentence was dangerous. It opened a door inside her head that until now had always been firmly locked. Images flooded her brain of him cradling a newborn baby, its downy head covered in ink-black hair, making something tighten around her heart like the slow closing grip of an invisible fist.

Izzy let out a measured breath to bring herself back under control. 'You really know how to kill a mood, don't you?' Her attempt at humour didn't quite hit the mark.

Andrea took one of her hands and pressed it to his mouth, his eyes still holding hers. 'It's an important conversation to have because this is only for six months. A child would change everything.'

'Rest easy, Andrea. I don't want to have kids. Do you have this conversation with every woman you sleep with?'

'I always use condoms. No exceptions.' A small frown pulled at his forehead. 'My relationships don't normally last longer than a few weeks, if that.'

'Why's that?'

He twirled a strand of her hair around one of his fingers, his gaze dropping to her mouth. 'I don't like giving my partners false hope. I'm not the settling down type. I bore too easily.'

'So you end things before they get too clingy?'

'Works for me.'

Izzy wondered why he had got to the age of thirty-four without wanting more than a few weeks of passion with yet another lover he would then let go without a backward glance. Didn't he want more than that?

Didn't she?

Izzy blocked the thought like slamming the door on an unwelcome guest. What she wanted was to buy back her grandparents' house to honour her mother's wishes. That was her goal and she was not going to rest until she achieved it. She touched his jaw again, moving beneath his weight, her body still on fire. 'Are we done talking now?'

His lips curved up at one corner, a glint in his eyes. 'What else did you have in mind?'

Izzy pulled his head down so his mouth was just above hers. 'Figure it out.'

His mouth covered hers in a kiss that triggered a wave of longing deep in her body. His hands moved over her in barely touching strokes that heightened her skin's awareness, ramping up her need to feel him crush her to him. He took his time pleasuring each erotic zone on her body—her breasts, the underside of her wrists, her thighs. He moved down her body, leaving kisses on her electrified flesh, teasing her into a frenzy of want that made her writhe and whimper. Clothes were removed and discarded, both his and hers, and for once she didn't feel naked and exposed and embarrassed.

He parted her thighs and stroked her with his fingers, making her snatch in a breath as the sensations tingled through her most tender private flesh. She had never allowed a partner to be so intimate with her. Not that her less than a handful of lovers had even tried. But Andrea's touch was so gentle, so respectful and giving she was swept away on the sheer eroticism of it, her inhibitions fading as tingles of pleasure shot through her in tiny little fizzes. His lips and tongue caressed her, opening her to a new world of feeling, a world of cataclysmic pleasure that left no part of her body untouched. Ripples of delight ran from her core to her extremities, even to her fingertips and toes. A shiver ran over her scalp, coursed down her spine and back up again as every muscle and tendon in her body shook and shuddered with a release so exquisite it blew every thought out of her mind.

Andrea stroked the side of her thigh as she came back to her senses. Izzy couldn't speak. Didn't want to speak in case she ruined the atmosphere by saying the wrong thing—an unsophisticated, self-conscious comment that would make him realise how disparate their lives were when it came to sex. She was in no doubt of his experience. Hadn't he just proven it? He had played her body like a maestro played a temperamental instrument. He had made her senses sing with such harmony and balance that she couldn't imagine ever allowing any other man to touch her now she had experienced his caresses.

Andrea brushed back her hair from her face, his gaze hooded but with a light of intensity—a probing light of contemplation. 'You've gone very quiet, *cara*.'

Izzy forced a smile. 'Don't you want to…?' She waved a hand to their where their bodies were pressed together. 'Finish off?'

He took her hand and pressed a kiss to the middle of her palm, his eyes still holding hers. 'There's no hurry. I want to savour every minute.'

Izzy chewed the side of her mouth, her gaze slipping out of reach of his. With her free hand she traced the carved contour of his left pectoral muscle with her finger. 'I've never slept with someone so…so not in a hurry…'

He brought her chin up with the end of his finger, locking his gaze on hers. There was a soft concerned look in his eyes that made her wonder if her enmity towards him had been misplaced, misguided, mishandled. 'Your pleasure is important to me. I want our first time together to be mutually satisfying, not a fast and furious fumble that leaves you frustrated.' His thumb brushed over her lower lip for a moment, his brow furrowing. 'Are you telling me you haven't always enjoyed sex?'

Izzy lost herself in the dark warmth of his gaze. How could he so easily read her mind? Her body? Her emotions? 'I'm not as experienced as I've made it appear or sound in the press.' She sighed and continued. 'I've never been all that comfortable with physical intimacy. I couldn't bear the thought of being intimate with anyone without numbing myself first with alcohol. None of my partners seemed all that interested in whether I was having a good time or not. Everyone assumed I was the up-for-it party girl, but in reality... Well, this is the first time I've had an orgasm with a partner. I used to fake it to get sex over with.'

He touched her face with a slow-moving finger from her cheek to her chin and back again. 'Oh, Isabella.' His voice had a soft note of compassion that derailed her even further. 'Sex is supposed to be a mutual thing, not a one-way street. Your partners should have checked to see if you were comfortable with what they were doing. You shouldn't have to endure sex but enjoy it.'

Izzy gave him a self-deprecating smile, so touched by his understanding she was worried she might get emotional. 'Speaking of one-way streets... Are you going to finish making love to me?'

The shadow of concern was back in his gaze. 'Is that what you want? What you *really* want?'

Izzy stroked his face from ear to stubbly jaw. 'I want you to make love to me. I want to experience your pleasure as well as my own.' Her voice was nothing more than a breathy whisper but it contained all the longing she felt for him, the longing she could feel throbbing, deep and heavy, in her blood.

He brought his mouth down to just above hers. 'Are you sure?' His warm breath caressed her lips and his hesitancy melted her heart.

'I'm sure,' she said and closed the gap between their mouths.

CHAPTER EIGHT

IZZY'S MOUTH WAS on fire as soon as Andrea's met hers. His tongue a flame of need that echoed her own. The mutual exchange of passion thrilled her, ramping up her excitement because with every sensuous touch and caress it erased the bad memories of the past. It was an awakening of her flesh, of her desire, of her ability to give and receive pleasure and she gloried in it.

Andrea was slow and thorough in attending to all her pleasure spots, leaving no secret place undiscovered. He kissed and stroked her breasts, nibbled and nudged and gently grazed them with his teeth so that every hair on her head was tingling at the roots.

But she was just as keen to explore him and ran her hands over his taut muscles and his steely flanks and his flat abdomen. She took him in her hands and learnt his likes and dislikes, reading him as he had read her and enjoying the way he responded to her touch. Feeling powerful in a way she had never felt before.

Andrea sourced a condom and positioned himself at her entrance. The final moment of physical connection was so strongly erotic and yet surprisingly tender, it took her breath clean away. Her body welcomed him, accepting him and wrapping around him with no fear, no reluctance and no pretence. The slow movement of him within her drew from her a fevered response as her nerves began to sing at the friction. She was climbing to a far off summit, each of her muscles becoming taut with built-up tension. She was not quite there and yet so close it was like hovering on the edge of a precipitous cliff.

Andrea brought his hands between their rocking bodies and caressed her intimately, his fingers cleverly stroking her over the edge into a free fall into the abyss. Her senses were reeling, spinning her away from conscious thought, her body a blissful array of sensations that rippled through every pore of her flesh. It was like her nerves were on the outside of her skin, every movement, every touch of his hands and body making her hum and throb with pleasure.

Izzy felt his release follow soon after. There was none of the huffing and grunting and crushing, almost suffocating weight of her previous partners. Andrea held her close and gave himself up to the moment of completion with a deep guttural groan that reverberated through her body as if his pleasure was intimately tied to hers. She felt every one of his spasms as if they were her own, making her feel closer to him than she had ever felt to anyone. Emotion suddenly clogged her throat, her eyes stinging with unshed tears. She lamented her lack of sophistication for feeling so exposed and vulnerable and hid her face against his neck, hoping he would put her silence down to her satiated senses.

After a minute or two of silence, Andrea propped himself up on his elbows and turned her head so she was facing him. His brows came together when he saw the glimmer of tears in her eyes. 'Did I hurt you?' His tone had a ragged edge that made the stitches around her heart loosen even more.

Izzy gave a lopsided smile. 'No, of course not. You were wonderfully gentle. It's just I…I didn't realise it could be that good. That satisfying and…not sleazy or rushed or shameful in any way.'

He mopped a couple of tears that had escaped from beneath her eyes, the look in his gaze so tender it made her want to cry all over again. She was used to partners rolling away and leaving. Job done. End of story. Andrea's approach was so different… so touchingly different it was like he had made love with not just her body but with her mind and soul.

'You were wonderful too,' he said. 'I always knew we would be good together.'

Izzy trailed her fingers down the hairy roughness of his forearm, her eyes avoiding his. 'Why wait so long to act on it?' She slowly brought her gaze up to his. 'I mean, for all this time we could have been making love instead of war.'

His smile was rueful and he captured a strand of her hair and tucked it back behind her ear. 'It's one of the reasons I've always kept my distance. I didn't trust myself around you. But my housekeeper, Gianna, knew I was beaten the minute she met you. Even before she met you.'

'Because I'm the first woman you've brought here?'

'Because you're the first woman I've married.'

Izzy glanced at the rings on her left hand. They looked so real and yet... An invisible hand fisted around her heart. This was for six months and six months only. He didn't want a wife any more than she wanted a husband. They weren't doing *for ever*. They were doing *for now*. For money. For mutual advantage. She brought her gaze back to his. 'But Gianna knows this is a marriage of convenience. We've both told her that none of this is real.'

He moved away to dispose of the condom. 'I told you—she's a die-hard romantic. A marriage of convenience to her means an opportunity to fall in love. She married her late husband to settle family debts and they had thirty-odd happy years together before he died a couple of years ago.' He glanced back at her but his expression was now masked. 'Don't let her get to you. We'll do it our way and when it's time to end it, we'll do so without tears. Agreed?'

Izzy didn't care for the slightly clinical tone he used. Surely this wasn't like any old business deal? This was about two lives intersecting, two bodies giving and sharing pleasure. She screened her own expression, hiding her niggling doubts behind a smile she wasn't sure made the distance to her eyes. 'Agreed.'

He leaned down to brush her mouth with a brief kiss, and then he straightened and reached for his trousers. 'I have to see to a couple of things in my office to do with my business merger. Will you be okay to entertain yourself for an hour or two? We'll have dinner out on the terrace. Maybe have a moonlight swim afterwards. I'll give Gianna the night off so we won't be disturbed.'

'Sounds like fun,' Izzy said, already tingling at the thought of sharing a moonlit swim with him.

An hour and a half later and Andrea still hadn't worked his way through the pile of paperwork sitting on his desk. His mind kept drifting back to making love with Izzy. He still couldn't believe he had crossed the boundary he'd been so adamant not to cross. But the things she had shared about her past and her insecurities had made it virtually impossible for him to resist her. A barrier had been removed between them and it had opened up a world of sensuality that until now he had been avoiding. Their lovemaking had been both tender and passionate and his body was still tingling from her touch. He knew it was dangerous to tweak the terms of their arrangement but he assured himself it was only for six months. Yes, a bit longer than his usual relationships, but they both stood to gain from the deal. His colleague's wedding was only a couple of weeks away and he figured now he was sleeping with Izzy it would make their marriage look all the more authentic.

It sure felt damn authentic, which was a thought he shouldn't be allowing inside his head. But he reassured himself that Izzy didn't want a long-term marriage any more than he did. They had both been clear from the outset on what they wanted out of this arrangement. She had far more to lose than he and he was counting on her abiding by the rules so she got what she wanted. Her inheritance. Which she *deserved*, for he firmly believed now she had been badly treated by her father. It angered Andrea that he had held her father in such high esteem when all the time Benedict had been manipulative and cruel towards Izzy. Andrea knew enough about her to know she was a lot more sensitive and soft-hearted than she let on. The brash don't-mess-with-me exterior was an act, a ruse to put people off so they wouldn't see how easily she could be hurt.

But making love with her had made Andrea realise how careful he would have to be not to end up hurting her himself. They had made an agreement. Six months. He wasn't interested in prolonging their relationship or indeed any relationship in the future. He had no desire to lay himself open to rejection again. To be shunted aside when feelings died. To be kicked out of someone's life as if he were nothing more than useless trash.

No. He would stick to the plan. Keep his emotions out of the arrangement and enjoy the physical chemistry he had going on with Izzy.

Stick to the plan.

That was all he had to do.

Izzy showered and came downstairs in time to receive instructions from Gianna about the heat and serve dinner she had prepared. A candlelit table with a crisp white tablecloth was set up on the terrace overlooking the pool and the Positano coastline below. Two cushioned chairs were positioned either side of the table and a gorgeous arrangement of fresh flowers was elegantly draped either side of the scented candles. It was the most romantic setting Izzy had ever seen and yet she couldn't help feeling a little conflicted. Making love with Andrea had changed something in their relationship. She didn't hate him. Her hatred had been her armour and now she was fighting a battle without a weapon. What defences could she use if not her dislike of him?

But how could she dislike someone who made her feel such magical things?

Her body was still alive with the sensations he'd evoked. She had only to think of his powerful body entering her and her stomach would flip over and a hot rush of longing course through her. It was dangerous to let her guard down but how could she not? They were tied together for six months and now they had this new intimacy she couldn't turn things back to the way they had been. A switch had been flicked. A force had been activated. A desire had been fed and fuelled and fostered.

Andrea came out to the terrace carrying a bottle of champagne. He too had recently showered, for his hair was still damp and curling around the collar of his casual shirt. Izzy hadn't seen him since they had made love but his office door had remained closed every time she'd walked past as she'd helped Gianna set up dinner before the housekeeper left for the evening.

Andrea's eyes ran over Izzy's oyster silk dress, the only decent thing she'd had time to slip into her overnight bag. 'You look beautiful. The rest of your things should be here by tomorrow. But we can shop for anything else you need.'

'Thanks.' Never good with compliments, Izzy feasted her eyes on him instead. The way his muscles bunched on his tanned forearms when he popped the champagne cork, the way his olive skin contrasted with the white of his shirt. Her gaze drifted to his mouth, remembering how it had felt on her own, how his tongue had mated with hers in such an erotic way. Something shivered deep and low in her belly when his eyes met hers. Was he remembering how it felt to be inside her? Was he thinking of how it had felt to be consumed by passion and want until nothing else mattered? She licked her suddenly dry lips and made a business out of straightening the perfectly straight tablecloth. 'It's a gorgeous night. So lovely and warm. I can't remember the last time I ate al fresco.'

He placed a warm hand on her bare shoulder, his touch sending a wave of longing through her body. 'You're nervous.' He said it with a note of surprise rather than as a question.

Izzy could feel her cheeks betraying her. 'I'm just not used to relating to you like this…you know, without biting your head off. It's kind of…weird. Weird but…nice.'

He gave a slow smile and leaned down to press a kiss to the sensitive flesh just below her ear. She could smell the fresh citrus of his aftershave, her senses intoxicated by lemon and lime and cleanly showered man. Even though he'd recently shaved she could still feel the slight prickle of his sexy stubble. His breath caressed her skin, then his tongue glided in a blistering pathway following the line of her jaw until he finally came to her mouth. His kiss was slow and sensual, lighting fires in her flesh that sent hot flames licking along her veins. Her mouth opened under the commanding pressure of his, her arms slipping around his neck, bringing her closer to the heat and hardness of his body. Her breasts were bare under her shoestring-strap dress and never had they felt more sensual than with the cool silk stretched over them as they were crushed against his muscular chest. His hands skimmed her from her shoulders to her hips, his hands settling there to bring her even closer against his pulsing need. She could feel her body preparing itself, excitement kicking up her heartbeat, making her intensely aware of every inch of her body where it was pressed against his.

His mouth continued its sensual exploration of hers, their tongues tangling in a sexy dance of one-upmanship that stirred her desire even more. His hands came back up to cradle her face as he changed position, his mouth softening against hers, his tongue no longer combative but cajoling.

Izzy had had no idea a kiss could be so mind-blowing, so thrilling that her whole body would be involved. Every nerve and cell throbbing with growing need—a need he activated and nurtured with each mesmerising movement of his mouth on hers. His hands splayed into her hair, electrifying her scalp with his touch.

He lifted his mouth off hers to look at her through sexily hooded eyes. 'This is a much better way to relate to each other, *si*?'

Izzy smiled against his mouth. 'Much better.'

He kissed her again, deeply, holding her against his aroused body while the scent of the flickering candle and the flowers and the sea air worked their magic on her senses.

Izzy felt like she had stepped into a fairy tale, one she had never realised she'd wanted until now: a romantic setting, a warm fragrant night, champagne and delicious food and a man who had eyes only for her.

What more could she want?

Andrea pulled back from her with a smile. 'We won't do the dinner Gianna has prepared for us service if we get distracted. Some champagne, *cara*? To celebrate our truce.'

'Yes, please.' Izzy held out her hand for the glass of sparkling bubbles he poured. He held out her chair and she sat and gazed at the view below. 'This is the most beautiful place. How long have you had it?'

He took his seat opposite. 'I bought it five years ago. I got sick of living in my hotels. I wanted a base, a place to separate me from work.' His lips moved in a rueful movement. 'Not that it always works that way. Gianna is always telling me off for spending way too much time in my office here.'

Izzy sipped her champagne and studied him for a moment over the rim of her glass. He looked far more relaxed than she had ever seen him. His shirt was undone to midway down his chest and the sleeves rolled up past his forearms. She wondered now why she'd found him so intimidating and gruff in the past. 'How did you get into hotels? Why not some other business?'

He handed her a crisp bread roll from the basket on the table between them. 'When I left home when I was fourteen—'

'Fourteen?' Izzy looked at him in alarm. 'You were fourteen when you left home?'

He gave her a grim smile that wasn't really a smile. 'Not by choice, although it was proving to be impossible to live with my stepfather.'

Izzy glanced at the scar on his left eyebrow, her stomach feeling queasy at what he might have been exposed to as a young boy. 'Is that how you got that scar? From your stepfather?'

He touched the scar as if to see if it was still there, a shadow passing over his expression as if the memories of that time in his life were unpleasant. 'He was a bastard of a man—a coward who used his fists instead of his intellect. Not that he had much of an intellect.' His tone was flat and bitter, the line of his mouth tight.

Izzy swallowed, remembering all too well how terrifying it was to live with a man with a hair trigger temper. 'Was he violent towards your mother?'

Andrea's dark eyes glittered and his jaw clenched. 'He was clever how he went about it. He didn't leave her with bruises you could see. I intervened whenever I could but in the end she chose to stay with him.' His mouth thinned into a white line. 'That's what hurt me the most. I came back the next day after he kicked me out and begged her to leave with me. I promised I'd keep her safe—find a shelter or something for us. But she told me she never wanted to see me again. She wanted to stay with my stepfather. Go figure.'

Izzy frowned, her heart squeezing at the thought of Andrea as a young teenager, thrown out of home and rejected by his mother. 'Oh, Andrea. How awful that must have been. You must have been so distraught. What did you do? Where did you go?'

He took a sip of his champagne, and then another sip, each time swallowing deeply. 'I lived on the streets for a couple of months until I met your father. He found me looking for food at the back of a hotel in Florence. The kitchen hand used to watch out for me and give me some leftovers.' Andrea's smile became crooked. 'Your father might not have been an angel, but if it hadn't been for him taking a chance on me, who knows where I might have ended up?'

It was certainly a side to her father Izzy had been aware of but the various charities and people he'd championed didn't make up for how he'd made her feel. 'How did he help you?'

'He found a place for me to stay and then offered me a job. It was menial work at first, just cleaning and stuff, but he said later my work ethic had impressed him.' He reached across and refilled her glass but she noticed he didn't refill his own. 'I went back to school and studied for a business degree after that. When I was living on the streets I made a promise to myself that one day I would own a hotel where the homeless would be welcome to find shelter and food.' He put the bottle back in the ice bucket and sat back in his chair. 'Enough about me. Tell me about Hamish. What was he like?'

Izzy wondered if anyone else knew the darker secrets of his past and felt touched he'd shared as much as he had with her. She could tell from his expression that he was not used to talking about his background at length. There was a shuttered look in his eyes as if he had cordoned off the memories and would not be revisiting them any time soon. 'Hamish was a lot older than me, as you know—my mother had a few miscarriages in between having him and me. But he was wonderful. Funny and smart—all the things a big brother should be. I idolised him and he spoilt me rotten. But then he got sarcoma and everything in our family changed. The much-adored son and heir couldn't be saved, no matter how much the doctors and my parents tried.' She let out a ragged sigh. 'It was a terrible time. As the years went on, my father expected me to step up and do all the things Hamish would have done if he'd lived. But I wasn't strong academically. I wasn't able to cope with the pressure and I rebelled.' She frowned at the memory of that difficult period in her life. 'I wish I'd had someone to talk to about it, but the sad irony was Hamish was the only person I would have shared something like that with but he was gone and so I floundered.'

'What about your mother? Were you close to her?'

Izzy always felt sad when she thought of her mother. Talking about her made her realise how much she still missed her. Missed what they'd once had before tragedy struck. 'I was close to her before Hamish got sick. We had a happy family until then, or so it felt from my young, childish perspective. It was happiest when my father wasn't around, though. That's why I loved going to my grandparents' house so much because Dad never came with us. He didn't get on with his in-laws. But then Hamish got sick and Mum was understandably devastated. She felt she'd failed as a mother, as a wife. Then my grandparents got killed in a car crash a couple of years later and Mum retreated further into herself and soon after she got liver cancer. It was like our family was cursed.'

Andrea's expression was full of concern and compassion. 'How did your father handle it all?'

Izzy puffed out her cheeks on another sigh. 'He worked. He went away a lot, which suited me because we only ever argued when he was around. He couldn't see me without making some cutting comment about how I was dressed or how badly I'd done in my latest test or how much I disappointed him with my behaviour. I used to dread him coming home, and yet often I would deliberately set him off because it was a way to get his attention. Immature, now that I think about it.'

'So you were never close to him? Even as a younger child?'

Izzy gave him a pained movement of her lips that was not quite a smile. 'He wasn't comfortable around little kids. He didn't understand their needs, or perhaps didn't want to. Mum let slip once that he was the same with Hamish until Hamish grew up a bit. But then, even when I got a bit older, I realised I would never be good enough because I wasn't a boy. It was all my father had ever wanted. A son to carry on the family line. I was close to my mother's parents, though. They were lovely to me and, of course, to Hamish.' She met his gaze. 'That's why I want my inheritance. I want to buy back their home. My father insisted it be sold after they were killed. My mother didn't want to sell it but he talked her into it.'

'Where is it?'

'In Wiltshire,' Izzy said. 'A few kilometres out from a quaint tiny village no one's ever heard of but to me it's like paradise. Some of my earliest and best memories are of being at my grandparents' house with Hamish and Mum. It was the happiest time of our lives. I won't rest until I get it back. The current owner has promised me they won't sell for another six months.'

'What will you do with it once you buy it? Will you live there?'

'That's the plan,' Izzy said. 'I have to iron out a few more details but I'd like to open it up as a short-term holiday place for families going through difficult times. Maybe even kids with cancer. There's a lovely little gardener's cottage that could be done up to house guests as well as the main house.' She picked up her bread roll and tore off a piece. 'I suppose it all sounds a little hare-brained to a hotshot hotel owner like you. It's not like I've got a business plan or anything. I haven't even been down to see the place in years.'

He reached for her hand and gave it a gentle squeeze. 'I started small and built up gradually. You've got passion about the project, which is far more important than anything else.'

Izzy glanced at their joined hands, her wedding and engagement rings winking up at her as if to remind her of the terms of their marriage. She pulled her hand away and went back to buttering her bread roll. 'Do you ever see your mother?' He was silent for so long she looked back up at him. 'Andrea?'

He blinked as if bringing himself back to the present. 'No.'

'Have you ever tried to make contact?'

'What would be the point?' There was a line of

hardness around his mouth that hinted at the bitterness he still carried about his childhood.

Izzy chewed her lip, wondering if she'd strayed into dangerous territory. 'I don't know... I just thought it might help you understand why she did what she did.'

'She made her choice. That's the end of it as far as I'm concerned.'

'But what if it hadn't been her choice?' Izzy met his black-as-pitch gaze. 'What if she was frightened of your stepfather? Of what he would do to her, to both of you, if she left with you? Maybe he forced her to tell you to go away and never come back.'

Something flickered over his face like ice cracking on the surface of a frozen lake. 'She's had plenty of time to find me if she was so inclined. I've not exactly been hiding under a rock.'

'But would you agree to see her if she did come looking?'

A cynical glint appeared in his eyes. 'And what do you think she'd want from me all these years on? Money?'

'I can understand why you'd feel so cynical about her motives but surely—'

'Isabella. Please, can we change the subject?' His matter-of-fact tone brooked no resistance. 'You have your father issues. I have my mother ones. Let's leave it at that.'

'But your mother might still be alive,' Izzy said, trying to ignore the jab of pain just below her heart. The pain of guilt and regret that it was now too late for her to make her peace with her father.

Andrea's eyes lost their glaze of hardness and he reached for her hand again. *'Cara...'* His voice was softer now, almost tender, his touch a soothing press of fingers against her hand that made her feel understood and supported. 'Forgive me. My stuff happened a long time ago. So long ago it feels like it happened to someone else, not me. But your grief is still fresh. Raw. Your father was wrong to make you jump through hoops. But he had his own issues. Unhappy people hurt others because it's a way of controlling them.'

Izzy forced a stiff little smile. 'I wonder what he'd think of you marrying me. Do you think he envisaged it might happen?'

He stroked his thumb over the back of her hand. 'Who knows? But the main thing is you get your inheritance once the six months is up.' He gave her hand a little Mexican wave-like tap with his fingers and withdrew his hand. 'Which reminds me—I have my business colleague's wedding coming up in two weeks. It's being held in Venice. It will be a glamorous affair so let me know if you'd like help choosing an outfit. I'll pay, of course.'

'You don't have to buy me clothes.'

He shrugged and reached for his champagne. 'Think of it as one of the perks of the deal. Any amount of money is worth spending when it gets you what you want.'

'Why do you want this business merger so much?' Izzy asked. 'You have lots of hotels now. What's so special about the one you're trying to buy?'

'The hotel in Florence is the one where your father found me begging for food. For years I've wanted that hotel and when I set my sights on something I don't give up until I achieve it.' The determined set to his mouth reminded her of his iron will and take-no-prisoners attitude. 'Patrizio Montelli's hotel is small by industry standards but I won't rest until I own it. But first I have to solve the issue of his stepdaughter.'

'I hope his stepdaughter buys our marriage as the real deal and not a sham,' Izzy said. 'I mean, for a man of your wealth and position, you did marry me rather quickly and with little or no fanfare.'

His eyes smouldered like coal as they held hers. 'Alexis will only have to take one look at us together to know what we have is real. You can't fake chemistry like ours.'

Izzy picked up her glass in case she was tempted to give in to that crackling chemistry right here and now. 'Are we going to do justice to this dinner Gianna made for us? It's probably getting cold.'

He gave a lazy smile. 'Dinner first and then a swim.'

'I haven't got a swimming costume with me.'

His eyes glinted. 'Trust me. You won't need one.'

CHAPTER NINE

AFTER THEY CLEARED away the remains of dinner Izzy followed Andrea back out to the pool. He turned off most of the garden lights for added privacy and the pool became bathed in moonlight, the surface perfectly still in the balmy evening air.

Andrea unbuttoned his shirt, giving her a smouldering look that made her insides quiver with longing. 'Have you ever skinny-dipped before?'

'No.' Izzy slipped one shoulder strap down. 'I seem to be having a few firsts with you.'

He removed the rest of his clothes and came to help her with hers. His hands were warm and sensual as they slid the other strap off her shoulder, the dress falling into a silken pool at her feet, leaving her with nothing but her knickers. His eyes devoured her naked breasts, his hands cupping them so gently it made every pore of her skin react. His thumbs brushed over her nipples, teasing them into tight buds, the flesh aching and tingling with a torturous longing. He brought his mouth down and stroked his tongue over the upper curve of each breast, his teeth taking each nipple in a soft bite that made her spine shiver. His tongue swirled around her nipple, a warm soothing stroke that sent a shockwave straight to her core. He peeled her knickers away and they too fell to her feet and she stepped out of them, desperate to press her body as close to his as possible.

The contact of his hard male body against hers made her womb contract with need—a tight, aching need that begged to be assuaged. It moved through every part of her body in a rolling tide, making her heart race and her breathing quicken. No one had ever made her feel desire like this. So powerful. So consuming. So enthralling.

Andrea bent down in front of her, bringing his mouth to her most intimate place. She placed her hands on his head to anchor herself, preparing for the tumultuous storm his lips and tongue promised. Izzy gave herself up to the sensations as his mouth continued its erotic exploration, the tension building in her body until finally it could take no more. She shattered around his tongue, gasping and shuddering as the ripples of pleasure coursed through her in cascading waves.

Andrea rose to gather her close, his hands warm

on her hips, his eyes backlit with desire. 'I love how you come apart when I do that. You're so responsive.'

Izzy reached up to touch his mouth with her finger. 'I never thought I'd ever feel comfortable enough to let anyone pleasure me like that.' She touched his lower lip and sighed. 'I can't imagine doing it with anyone else...'

Something flickered in his gaze as quick as a jab of pain. But then his gaze relaxed but somehow his smile didn't match. 'I promised you a swim. Let's do it.' He stepped away from her and dived into the deep end of the pool, his lean athletic body slicing through the water, sending rippling waves to the edges, not unlike the ones he had sent through her body moments earlier.

Izzy stood on the edge of the pool, hesitant to dive because there was no way she could do it as expertly as Andrea. She watched him swim up and down, privately envying the way he executed deft tumble turns at each end as if he were at an Olympic training session. He reminded her of her brother, Hamish, who had been an excellent swimmer. But the swimming gene hadn't come her way, which was another thing her father had berated her for, to such a degree she hadn't swum in years.

Andrea surfaced and flicked his wet hair back with one of his hands. 'Come on. It's not cold.'

Izzy went to the shallow end where the steps were and cautiously entered the water, only going waist-deep. The water was like warm silk against her naked skin, making her aware of every inch of her body. 'I'll just have a paddle up this end,' she said.

He joined her at the shallow end, his gaze searching hers. 'What's wrong? Don't you like swimming?'

Izzy gave a self-conscious grimace. 'I'm not a great swimmer. Hamish was but I didn't share his natural talent.'

Andrea frowned. 'Did your father make unhelpful comparisons?'

She marvelled at his ability to read between the lines whenever she spoke of her childhood. 'It took all the enjoyment out of it to have my father standing by the side of the pool telling me what I was doing wrong.'

His hands took hers, his expression gentle with concern. 'He was a hard taskmaster. He expected perfection and got frustrated when people didn't measure up. But he should never have treated you like that. No one should be treated like that and especially not a child.'

Izzy moved closer to him, her arms going around his waist, her pelvis in intimate contact with his.

'Thank you for understanding. I know it must be hard to see my father with new eyes. I know he was good to you. He was good to a lot of people. He just wasn't able to be the sort of father I needed.'

He brushed her forehead with his lips. 'I'm grateful for what he did for me. But I wasn't as close to him as he made out. I wasn't close to anyone.' He let out a brief sigh and added, 'I'm still not.'

What about me? Her unspoken question seemed to hover in the air between them. Didn't he feel close to her? She had told him stuff she had told no one. He had shared things about his past she was sure he had not revealed to anyone else. They had shared their bodies with such breathtaking intimacy. What would it take for him to lower his guard enough to feel close to her?

Izzy stroked her hands over the small of his back, feeling his tense muscles relax at her touch. 'I guess it would be hard to be close to anyone after being deserted by your mother,' she said. 'How could you trust anyone after that?'

His lips moved in the semblance of a smile and his gaze went to her mouth. 'Hey. I thought we came down here to swim?'

Izzy gave him a sultry smile. 'Do you really want to swim?'

His eyes darkened with desire and he brought his mouth closer to hers. 'Not right now.'

The next two weeks passed in a sensual haze that Izzy never wanted to come out of even though she knew at some point she must. It was always lurking at the back of her mind that none of this was going to last—that this dream of living with Andrea at his gorgeous villa on the Amalfi coast was temporary. No amount of Izzy's words to the contrary could convince his housekeeper, Gianna, to believe Izzy's marriage to Andrea wouldn't magically turn into the real thing. Gianna smiled knowingly every time she saw Izzy coming out of the master bedroom and Izzy had to remind herself that, no matter how passionate his lovemaking, Andrea was not in love with her and didn't want their marriage to last any longer than it needed to in order to fulfil the terms of her father's will.

As for her feelings about him… Izzy sighed and tried not to think about how much she enjoyed being with him. Thinking too much made her want too much. Want things she hadn't even realised she wanted. Had never wanted until now.

But for now she tried to be content about being in a relationship that was mutually satisfying, not just physically but intellectually. He never made her feel she was a high school dropout. He engaged in debates and discussions with her about current affairs and, while he didn't always agree with her on every topic, he never made her feel embarrassed or foolishly naïve for holding a different view.

Andrea somehow juggled his demanding work while leaving enough time available to spend time with her. He took her shopping for clothes and took her to wonderful local restaurants where the food was as divine as his company. On Gianna's days off Izzy took over the cooking and, again mentally apologising to her feminist self, actually relished every moment of preparing meals for him as if she were channelling a nineteen-fifties housewife.

The day before they were to leave for Andrea's business colleague's wedding in Venice, Izzy woke during the night to the familiar twinge of period pain. Not wanting to wake Andrea, she quietly slipped out of bed and into the en suite bathroom, where she'd left some tampons in her toiletries bag. There was no paracetamol in her toiletries or her tote bag, so she went downstairs to the kitchen to a first aid cupboard where she had seen Gianna take out a Band-Aid a couple of days ago. She found the tablets and poured herself a glass of water and swallowed the pills, hoping it wouldn't be too long before they kicked in.

But as she stood looking out at the moonlit view over the coast she felt a strange twinge of disappointment. She placed a hand on her cramping abdomen and allowed a thought to slip under the locked door in her brain. The thought of carrying Andrea's child—a child conceived in love, not just in lust. A child they would raise as a married couple, invested in their relationship, not for material gain or to fulfil the terms of a will but because they truly loved each other and wanted to bring up a family together.

Izzy's hand fell away from her stomach. She was being silly allowing such a thought to take a foothold. What on earth would she do with a baby? She had never even held one. She didn't know the first thing about being a mother. She had watched her mother struggle all through her childhood to stand up for herself let alone her children. Who was to say Izzy would be any better at motherhood than she had been at anything else? She hadn't even completed school. What sort of mother would she make?

'*Cara?*' Andrea's deep voice shocked her out of her reverie. 'What are you doing down here at this time of night?' His gaze went to the paracetamol packet still lying on the kitchen bench. 'Are you unwell?' He came up close and placed a gentle hand on her forehead. 'You do look a little flushed but I don't think you've got a temperature.'

Izzy dipped away from the press of his hand and crossed her arms over her stomach. 'It's nothing. I just needed some paracetamol.'

He was still frowning. 'Do you have a headache?'

'No.' She let out a tight breath. 'Period cramps.'

He placed his hands on the tops of her shoulders. 'What can I do for you?'

Fall in love with me…

Izzy was terrified he would see the longing in her eyes so kept hers averted. 'Nothing. I've taken the painkillers so it'll ease soon enough.'

He brought up her chin with his finger. 'You should have woken me, *mio piccolo*. Do you often have painful periods?'

Izzy was aware of a thickness building in her throat—emotion that threatened to spill over the sandbags of her self-control. His tender care reminded her of all she would be missing out on once their marriage was over. Who had ever held and comforted her while she had period pain? Who had ever comforted her and looked at her with such concern? She blinked a couple of times and swallowed. 'Now and again.' She forced her lips into a stoical smile. 'I'll be fine, Andrea. You can go back to bed. I'll come up in a minute.'

He cradled her cheek with one of his hands, his eyes dark and intense as they held hers. 'Can I get you a hot pack? I'm sure Gianna has one some-where.'

'Please don't fuss.' Izzy pulled out of his hold and put some distance between them.

'Stop pushing me away, Isabella. I'm concerned about you.' His tone was still gentle but underpinned with a hint of frustration.

Izzy turned to the sink and poured herself another glass of water, chancing a sideways glance at his frowning features. 'You should be feeling relieved.'

'Why's that?'

She turned and waved a hand in front of her belly. 'I'm not pregnant.'

Something flickered over his face. 'Were you con-cerned you might be?'

Izzy shrugged. 'Not really.'

There was a loaded silence, as if he was thinking through an alternative scenario—the one she had been thinking about moments earlier. Was he imag-ining her belly growing round and heavy with their child? Was he picturing a dark-haired, dark-eyed baby with chubby limbs and tiny dimpled fingers?

Andrea cleared his throat and sent his fingers through his bed-tousled hair. 'I'll get you that heat pack.' He turned and went to a drawer at the other end of the kitchen and took out a microwavable pack and placed it in the microwave. 'Go up to bed. I'll be up with it in a couple of minutes.'

Izzy turned to leave the room, but when she glanced back from the doorway he was standing staring fixedly at the heat pack as he turned on the turntable.

Andrea took the heat pack out of the microwave and frowned. Izzy was right. He should be feeling relieved. Damn it. He *was* relieved. Incredibly relieved. The last thing he wanted to do was get her pregnant. A pregnancy would change everything. He didn't want that. Too many things had already been changed and he was only just keeping control. He was happy with how things were going. They were enjoying their relationship. But that didn't mean he wanted it to last any longer than the time they'd agreed on. He was keeping his emotions out of this. Wasn't he? Of course he was. He wasn't in any danger of blurring the boundaries.

Was Izzy relieved at not being pregnant? He had scrutinised her features but she was good at hiding her feelings. Better than he was at times. She was twenty-five years old. Was she hearing the tick-tock of her biological clock? She had told him she didn't want kids, but would she change her mind? It was a big issue. A life-changing issue that had to be thought about carefully. It was an issue he had thought about years ago and never revisited. Why would he? He had no knowledge of what a happy family looked like. His 'family' had been a disaster from the get-go. His biological father hadn't stayed around long enough to welcome Andrea into the world. His stepfather—one of a few over the years— had shown no interest in him other than as a punching bag. In theory, Andrea quite liked the idea of a loving and happy family but it was so rarely what happened in practice. He had decided it was easier, less painful, to move through life without the emotional encumbrances of a wife and children.

He refused to think of how lonely it might be once Izzy and he moved on with their lives.

He was used to being alone.

He'd been alone for most of his life.

Andrea took the heat pack upstairs to the master bedroom. Izzy was lying on her side with her head resting on one hand, her other hand pressed against her abdomen. There was an almost wistful cast to her features but when he approached she blinked and gave him a twisted smile. 'Sorry to have ruined your beauty sleep.'

He sat beside her on the bed and placed the heat pack against her belly. He used his other hand to brush her hair back from her forehead. 'Have those painkillers kicked in yet?'

'A little...'

Andrea traced his finger down the curve of her cheek. 'Will you be okay to come to Venice with me tomorrow for Patrizio Montelli's wedding?'

She turned over so she was lying on her back and held the heat pack against her stomach. 'Of course. It's just a period, Andrea. I've been having them every month since I was thirteen.'

He gave a wry smile. 'And here I was thinking shaving every day was a pain.'

She reached up and touched his jaw with her fingertips, her gaze going to his mouth. The tingle of her touch made every nerve in his body stand to attention. Her fingers were so soft, as light as a dove's feather brushing his skin, and yet they created a storm of fervent longing in his flesh. He captured her hand and brought it to his mouth, kissing each fingertip as he held her gaze. 'You should try and get some sleep.' His voice came out so husky it was as if his vocal cords had been rasped with a steel file.

Her eyes met his, her teeth snagging her lower lip. 'Andrea?'

He gave her hand a soft squeeze. 'Yes, *cara*?'

She opened her mouth to speak but then closed

it again, her eyes slipping away from his. 'Never mind...'

He inched up her chin and locked his gaze on hers. 'Is something troubling you, *mio piccolo*? The wedding tomorrow? There might be press there but I'll try and—'

'No, it's not about that.'

'What, then?'

She let out a gust of breath and her mouth moved in a vestige of a smile that looked sad rather than anything else. 'Nothing... I'm just feeling a little emotional, I guess. Hormones.' She lowered her gaze and began to pluck at the sleeve of his bathrobe as if she needed something to do with her hands.

Andrea bent down and pressed a soft kiss to the middle of her forehead. 'I can sleep in one of the spare rooms if you'd like? It might help you sleep better.'

Her hand gripped his arm. 'No. Please don't do that. I...' She moistened her lips with the tip of her tongue, her gaze shimmering. 'Would you just... hold me?'

Andrea slipped into bed beside her and gathered her close, his head resting on the top of hers as she nestled into his chest. Her silky hair tickled his chest and her body curled up so close made him feverishly aware of every place where it touched his. Her breathing slowly settled and he stroked the back of her head as if he were soothing a child. He couldn't remember a time when he had held someone in such an intimate embrace. Not sexually intimate, but with an emotional honesty he found strangely moving.

A faint alarm bell sounded in his head but he disregarded it. He wasn't getting *too* close to Izzy. They were both clear on the rules of their marriage. She was just feeling a little emotional due to hormones and he was comforting her. That was what any decent man would do, right? He wasn't falling in love with her. That was a line he was never going to cross.

Not with Izzy.

Not with anyone.

Izzy sighed and made a sleepy murmur and then turned over so her back was towards him, her legs in a sexy tangle with his and her neat bottom pushed up against his groin. Andrea wrapped his arms around her, enjoying the feel of her spooning against him. His hand held the heat pack to her stomach, and then, when it lost its warmth, he replaced it with his hand. Her stomach was flat but a thought crept into his head—of her belly slowly expanding as it accommodated a baby. *His* baby. He pushed away the thought but it kept coming back like smoke curling under a locked door. He had never pictured himself as a husband, much less a father. Having children was what other people did. Whenever he walked past families he thought, *Not for me*. It was an automatic response and he had never questioned it.

But now, holding Izzy in his arms with his hand pressed against her abdomen, he wondered why he was feeling this vague sense of emptiness. Like something was missing from his life but he wasn't sure what it was. Maybe it was the merger still hanging over him. Once that was sorted he would feel more balanced.

More in control.

And right now a little more control was exactly what he needed.

CHAPTER TEN

WHEN IZZY WOKE the next morning Andrea was already up and showered. He brought her a cup of tea and some toast on a tray and sat on the edge of the bed as he set it across her lap. 'How are you feeling this morning, *cara*?'

'Much better, thanks.' She took the cup of tea and cradled it in her hands. 'Thanks for taking such good care of me. It's a long time since I was cosseted like that.'

He gave her leg a little pat. 'You deserve to be cosseted. I was worried about you.'

'It would have been far more worrying if I hadn't got my period.' Izzy brought the cup to her mouth to take a sip of her tea.

'True.' He gave an on-off smile but a frown flickered across his brow.

There was a silence.

Izzy put her cup back on the tray. 'What time do we leave for Venice?'

He rose from the bed. 'Our flight leaves in about an hour or so. It's a late afternoon wedding so there'll be plenty of time to dress at the hotel before the service.'

'Will it be a big wedding?'

'Big enough.'

Izzy tilted her head at him. 'You're not looking forward to it, are you?'

He gave her another brief smile. 'Let's put it this way: I'll be glad when today is over.'

They arrived at their hotel in Venice—one of Andrea's smaller ones, but for all that no less gorgeous. Izzy freshened up her make-up and hair and then dressed in one of the outfits Andrea had bought her when they'd gone shopping a few days ago. It was navy blue satin that clung to her figure like a glove and she teamed it with a matching satin wrap and high heels.

Just as she was about to put on some costume jewellery, Andrea came over to her carrying a jewellery box. 'These are for you,' he said.

Izzy opened the box to find a stunningly beautiful sapphire and diamond pendant and matching droplet earrings nestled in a bed of luxurious velvet. 'Oh, my goodness…they're gorgeous.' She glanced up at him but his expression was difficult to read. 'You really shouldn't have spent so much money.'

He shrugged as if spending thousands and thousands of euros on designer jewellery was no big deal. 'You need to look the part at Patrizio and Elena's wedding.'

Izzy felt a sharp pang of disappointment like a needle stab to her heart. He hadn't bought the jewellery specifically for her but as a stage prop to convince everyone their marriage was not the sham it really was. She looked back down at the earrings and pendant, touching the shimmering diamonds with one of her fingers. 'You have excellent taste in jewellery...' Then she frowned and looked up at him again. 'But I thought you said you never bought your lovers jewellery?'

He took the box from her and removed the pendant. 'I don't. But this is different. Turn around and I'll put it on for you.'

Different? In what way? Did it mean he was beginning to care for her? To really care for her?

To feel *close* to her?

Izzy turned and lifted the back of her hair out of the way so he could fasten the pendant around her neck. The brush of his fingers against her skin made her shiver as if he had sent a current of electricity through her body. Once the pendant was in place she turned back around to face him. 'Why is it different?'

His gaze drifted to her mouth and back to her eyes

but his expression was still as inscrutable as ever. 'You're my wife. People will expect you to be wearing nice jewellery.'

Izzy touched the pendant hanging around her neck. 'But I'm only a temporary wife. Spending heaps of money seems a little over-the-top, given the circumstances.'

His mouth tightened for the briefest moment as if her comment had landed like a punch. 'No one knows this is temporary but us.'

'And Gianna.'

He gave a grunt that could have been agreement or scorn or both. 'I'm starting to wonder if I should have let her in on the secret.' He picked up his jacket and shrugged it on. 'You look beautiful, by the way. That colour suits you.'

Izzy smoothed down the front of her dress, ridiculously thrilled by his compliment. 'Thank you.' She picked up the earrings and inserted them into her ears. 'Will I do?'

His dark gaze ran over her like a minesweeper and he gave her a bone-melting smile. 'You'll more than do.'

The Montelli wedding service was conducted at St Mark's Basilica in Venice and Izzy took her assigned seat near the front on the groom's side while Andrea went forward to stand with Patrizio at the altar as his best man. The front of the church was beautifully adorned with flowers and each pew draped with white ribbons and bows and more garlands of flowers. A boy soprano choir sang with such exquisite scalp-tingling perfection, Izzy had tears sprouting in her eyes and a thickness developing in her throat. If she had been the type to imagine a dream wedding, then this would have been close to it. It was a painful reminder of how cold and impersonal her wedding ceremony to Andrea had been. It had been little more than a business transaction and, while their relationship had improved over the last couple of weeks, it didn't erase the fact that their marriage was not for ever.

The organist began playing the Wedding March and the congregation audibly drew in a collective breath when the bridesmaids—led by Patrizio's stepdaughter Alexis—came up the aisle. Dressed in the softest shade of rose, each bridesmaid carried a posy of tea roses and the cute little flower girl, who was only about three years old, carried a little basket of rose petals, but she proved too shy to do much other than hold her head down and clutch the hand of the nearest bridesmaid.

And then it was time for the bride to enter the church. Izzy turned and watched Patrizio's bride

Elena walk up the aisle in a wedding dress that was like something out of a fairy tale. With a lace bodice and long sleeves and a full skirt with a partial train and a voluminous veil, Elena glowed with beauty and happiness.

Izzy tried to suppress the pangs of envy but the closer the bride got to her beaming-with-pride groom, the worse she felt. It was as if someone was crushing her heart inside her chest when she thought of her own wedding day. Her travesty of a wedding ceremony with its impersonal witnesses and cynical seen-it-all-before marriage celebrant. The ceremony where no feelings were involved, no future planned, no promises of forever.

Just words without meaning, without conviction and commitment.

She glanced at Andrea but he was concentrating on his role as best man, although Izzy noticed Alexis casting him covert glances and blushing. The teenager reminded Izzy of herself at that age—awkward, not quite an adult and yet not really a child. Caught in a weird limbo with hormones and urgings but without the maturity to deal with them.

It was a painful reminder of all the mistakes Izzy had made in trying to get her father's attention.

So many mistakes. Mistakes she was still paying for now.

The service began and the bride and groom exchanged heartfelt vows. Izzy swallowed a lump in her throat as the bride and groom kissed. Andrea's eyes met hers and Izzy gave him a smile that was so tight it felt like her mouth would crack.

By the time the bridal procession left the church and the official photos were taken it was over an hour before Izzy got anywhere near Andrea. She felt like an extra on a film set. Not important enough to be in the main cast, just a walk-on figure.

But that was exactly what she was in Andrea's life. A walk-on part. A temporary bride who had no hope of a more permanent role. How could she have agreed to such an arrangement when she could have had what Patrizio and Elena had? No one looking at the new bride and groom could be in any doubt of their feelings for each other. Real feelings. Genuine feelings, not pretend.

Why couldn't Andrea look at *her* like that?

Izzy met his gaze during the reception and tried to fool herself he *was* looking at her like that, but then she realised he was acting the role of devoted husband. It was a jarring echo of what her father used to do. Pretending. Playing to an audience. There was nothing genuine about her relationship with Andrea, apart from the desire they shared. But how soon would that burn out for him? He was known for only staying with a lover for a month or so. She had been with him a little over two weeks. Would she be able to hold his interest for another five and a half months? How could she live with him, pretending she was happy with how things were?

She wasn't happy.

How could she be when all she had ever wanted was to be loved for who she was? Accepted and valued, not expected to be someone she could never be. Could she really pretend she was fine with how things were for another few months and then smile and wave goodbye when it was over? Didn't Andrea want more than a six-month affair? Especially after all they had shared both physically and emotionally? She had fooled herself he was getting close to her. He had shared his painful past, as she had shared hers.

Didn't that mean he felt something for her that he hadn't felt for anyone else?

The reception was being held at a private villa along the canals. The bridal party were transported in gondolas, but again Izzy felt on the outside, arriving on foot and having to sit with people she didn't know because Andrea was on the top table.

During the reception Andrea introduced her to Patrizio and Elena and Alexis, holding Izzy close to his side and smiling down at her with every appearance of being madly in love, but Izzy felt even

more conflicted. More of a fraud. More of a misfit.
More miserable. Every smile he sent her way made
her heart contract. Every touch of his made something in her stomach plummet in despair because
she knew the truth even if the wedding party and
guests did not.

Andrea didn't love her. If he did wouldn't he have
said so? Wouldn't he have taken the time limit off
their relationship? Wouldn't he have at least hinted
that things had changed for him? That his feelings
had changed?

'Is everything all right, *cara*?' Andrea asked,
drawing Izzy to one side during the last stages of
the reception.

'We need to talk.' Izzy kept her frozen smile in
place in case any wedding guests were watching.

He cupped her face, his brown eyes dark with
concern. 'Tired? Sorry it's been such a long day for
you. We can't leave until the bride and groom go,
but it won't be long now.'

Izzy couldn't bear for another minute to go past
without telling him how she felt. She looked up into
his eyes and tried to keep hers from tearing up. 'I
can't do this, Andrea. I just can't.'

His hands took her gently by the upper arms.
'Are you still unwell? I'm sorry, I should have asked
earlier.'

Izzy moved out of his hold and stepped further into the quiet alcove they were in. She crossed her arms over her body, suddenly chilled although the night was warm. 'I'm not sick. I'm just sick of pretending. I can't do it. It feels wrong to be fooling everyone our relationship is something it's not and never will be.'

A flicker of annoyance passed over his features. 'Can't this wait until we get back to our hotel?'

Izzy stood her ground, facing him with what was left of her pride. 'Did you feel *anything* during that wedding ceremony today? Anything at all?'

His expression tightened into a mask of steel. 'Isabella. This is not the time or place for this discussion.'

'I asked you a simple question.'

'And I told you I am not going to discuss this here.' His tone was so cold she felt another shiver pass over her flesh.

'I'll tell you how I felt. I felt guilty,' Izzy said. 'Guilty and disappointed and ashamed because I agreed to marry you for all the wrong reasons. I looked at Elena and Patrizio at the ceremony and saw two people who love each other. I want that. I want what they have.'

He frowned. 'You want us to have a formal ceremony? Is that what you're saying? You want a big

fancy church wedding even though we've only got
a few more months to the—'

'You don't get it, do you?' Izzy's heart felt as if it
were being pulverised, along with her pride. 'It's not
about having a big flashy wedding, Andrea. I want a
genuine marriage, one where there isn't a clock ticking. One where there isn't pretence and lying and
acting but real feelings. Feelings that last a lifetime.'

'No one can guarantee that.' His lips barely moved
over the clipped words. 'You can't. I can't.'

'Maybe not, but I'd still like to try.'

The silence was so thick it was like a suffocating fog.

Andrea let out a long slow breath but there was
no reduction of tension in his expression. 'You're
asking for something I can't give. We agreed on six
months. I've told you what I'm prepared to give and
a long-term commitment isn't part of it.'

She searched his gaze, desperately hoping to see
a flicker of warm emotion instead of clinical indifference. 'But why isn't it? Why is committing to
someone so difficult for you?'

He opened and closed his mouth as if carefully
monitoring his choice of words before he spoke. 'I'm
not prepared to discuss this now. We agreed on the
terms and—'

'I should never have agreed,' Izzy said. 'But I

wanted my grandparents' house so much it was all I could think about. But I realise now I want something else so much more. I can't spend another minute of my life trying to be what other people want or expect me to be. I have to be me. I have to be true to myself. For most of my life I thought I never wanted to be married. I can't believe I told myself such lies and for so long. But what I realise now is what I didn't want was my parents' marriage. My father didn't love my mother. If he'd loved her he wouldn't have tried to control her and squash her spirit.'

'I have no interest in trying to control you or squash your spirit, so please don't insult me by comparing me to your father,' Andrea said through tight lips.

'But you don't love me, do you?' Izzy felt as if she were stepping off a tall building into mid-air by asking such a question.

Every muscle on his face looked like it was having a spasm. Tension rippled along his jaw, his gaze as shuttered as a boarded-up window. 'That wasn't part of the bargain,' he said in a voice so devoid of emotion he could have been a robot.

Izzy knew she had been asking for the impossible but still she had clung to hope. But that fragile hope was now in the final throes of survival, gasping for air even as death crept inexorably closer. 'I don't want a business contract for a relationship. I don't want a bargain drawn up with terms and conditions and rules. I just want what most people want. Love. Commitment.'

'Look, we'll go back to our hotel and once you've had a good night's sleep you'll see this differently in the morning,' he said in a more conciliatory tone. 'You're tired and emotional.'

Izzy knew if she went back to the hotel with him she would end up in bed with him. She would end up going back to Positano with him and would spend the next five months hoping he would change his mind. She had spent too much of her life hoping for things she couldn't have. She had to be strong. She had to stand up for what she wanted. She owed it to herself. She couldn't live by someone else's agenda any longer. 'I'm not going back with you, Andrea. Not to your hotel. Not to your villa. It's over. We are over because we were never together in the first place.'

His eyes flinched as if too bright a light had struck him in the face. But then his expression turned to stone. 'Are you doing this deliberately?' He waved his hand towards the reception they could hear in the other room. 'Is this what you planned? To jeopardise everything I've worked so damn hard for?'

Izzy let out a sigh. 'That you would even think that proves how little you know me. I'm sorry if this ruins your merger but I consider my needs just as important as a business deal. I can't pretend to be happy with what we agreed on. I'm not happy. I could never be happy with someone who is unable to love me.'

'Are you saying you love me?' His frown was so heavy it made him look angry rather than confused.

Izzy considered telling him of her feelings for him but knew it wouldn't change anything. She had to keep some measure of pride. To offer her heart to him, only to have him hand it back with a *Thanks, but no thanks* would be too painful. 'I'm saying I want more than you can give me.'

'If you loved me, then you'd accept whatever I offered you,' he said. 'You'd accept it and be grateful because without me you're going to lose every penny of your inheritance.'

Izzy wondered how she could have ever thought that money would have been enough. Twice or thrice the amount wouldn't be enough in exchange for a loveless life. She only had to think of her mother to be reminded of how empty such a life could be. Even her dream of buying back her grandparents' estate seemed a pointless mission. What she had been trying to buy back was her happiness—the happiness she had once felt and longed to feel again.

But she wouldn't do it—*couldn't* do it—if it compromised her sense of self. Her sense of worth.

'I won't live with you under those terms, Andrea,' Izzy said. 'I'd be little more than a paid mistress, waiting for you to call time on our affair. I want to be an equal partner in a relationship. Not a pawn on a chessboard.'

'Your father was the one who put you on the chessboard, not me.' His lips were so flat they turned white. 'You should be grateful I was prepared to step in to help you. No one else was going to.'

'Is that what I'm supposed to feel? Grateful?' Izzy threw him an embittered glare. 'For what, exactly? That you fancied me? But how long is it going to last? Another week or two? A month? You don't stay with a lover longer than a few weeks. I can't live like that. I *won't* live like that.'

'Go, then.' He jerked his head towards the exit. 'Leave, and see how far it gets you. You'll be crawling back to me, begging me to take you back, before a day goes past.'

'I don't think you're listening to me, Andrea.' Izzy underscored her tone with a thread of steel. 'I'm not going to change my mind. I've finally grown up, like you told me to do all those years ago. I know what I want and I won't settle for anything less.' She forced herself to hold his unfathomable gaze. 'I'm going to collect my wrap and my purse from the reception and unless you want to create a scene that will be splashed over every newspaper and turn your friend's wedding into more of a farce than ours, then I suggest you let me leave without a fuss.'

One side of his mouth tipped up in a cynical curl. 'Blackmail, *cara*?'

Izzy raised her chin. 'You'd better believe it.'

CHAPTER ELEVEN

ANDREA DIDN'T BELIEVE IT. *Refused* to believe it. How could she walk away from her inheritance? How could she walk away from more money than most people saw in ten lifetimes?

How could she walk away from him?

His feelings were as raw as when he'd been a kid of fourteen, kicked to the kerb as if he was worth nothing. It freaked him out how similar the feelings were. Feelings he had spent a lifetime avoiding. He'd taught himself not to need people because he didn't want to feel like this.

Empty.

Blindsided.

Gutted.

He'd barely been able to speak to Izzy without betraying how shocked and disappointed he felt. He hadn't seen it coming. She couldn't have picked a worse time to drop that on him. He hadn't been prepared for her sudden bombshell. He'd fooled himself she wouldn't jeopardise her inheritance. Fooled himself that what they had together was…was what? More lasting?

No.

He didn't do forever. It wasn't on his radar. *Short-term and simple* was his credo. He had made no promises. He had made it clear right from the start he didn't want the complication of a long-term relationship. He accepted that it worked for other people but he didn't want it for himself. How could he when he had seen first-hand—*felt* first-hand—the blunt blow of rejection?

What was Izzy thinking? She had too much at stake to pull out now. They were only two weeks into their marriage. They had months left. Months and months he'd been looking forward to far more than he should. He'd known it was dangerous to get close to her. Known it and done it anyway, and now she had walked away. Thrown him over for what? She couldn't inherit without him.

She was calling his bluff—that was what this was. How could it be anything else? It was an attention-seeking tantrum to make him confess something he hadn't confessed to anyone and never would. The wedding had got to her. It was a grand and romantic affair that would have got to anyone. Even he'd felt a twinge or two of envy over Patrizio and Elena's commitment to each other.

But that didn't mean he wanted it for himself. He was happy with how things were. He and Izzy had been getting on so well. Their relationship was working the way he'd hoped it would—mutually satisfying, exciting and passionate.

And close...

Yes, well, that was the problem right there, wasn't it? He'd allowed her too close. Way too close. He'd been blinded by the intimacies they'd shared, not just the physical but the emotional. He had got to know her, the real Izzy, not the wild child façade she put on as a form of armour. Getting close to her, knowing her more deeply, had brought out the protector in him. She was the first woman he'd allowed close enough to stir that in him. Close enough to see his pain and shame over his troubled past.

But would she go through with her threat to walk away? There was no way she would walk out on him in the middle of his colleague's wedding. She knew how much was at stake, and not just for him but also for her. Was this her way of exacting revenge? Was that what she was doing? Making him pay for forcing her into marriage? But that didn't fit well with his new understanding of her. She wasn't a brash pay-you-back type. She was impulsive and feisty and, yes, a little sensitive and emotional, but those were the things he'd come to admire about her.

He'd thought they were getting on just fine. He'd thought their relationship was going exactly the way he'd wanted it to. They enjoyed each other's company. They were good together. Better than good—amazing. They'd shared the best sex he'd ever had and he'd looked forward to it continuing for another few months.

Anger coiled in his belly, tight and terrible anger mixed up in a toxic stew of disappointment and an even more disquieting sense of dismay. He was not the sort of man to feel dismayed or distraught. He hadn't felt like that since he was a teenager without a home, without a family.

Without anyone.

He never allowed anyone the opportunity to hurt him the way he'd been hurt back then. Izzy was probably still feeling a little hormonal. She would cool off in an hour or so and realise what was at stake for her and rethink her decision. By the time he got back to their hotel tonight she would be tucked up in bed and waiting for him.

He was counting on it.

Izzy only stayed at Andrea's hotel long enough to collect her passport and her overnight bag. She booked an early-morning flight back to London and moved into another hotel so she wouldn't encounter Andrea. How could she spend another night with him, knowing he didn't love her? Would never love her? Refused to love her? As much as she wanted him, it would be emotional suicide to continue to sleep with him. Even if he came back now and said he loved her, how could she be sure he wasn't pretending? Hadn't she heard her father say it numerous times without once meaning it?

Izzy barely slept that night and got to the airport early and boarded her flight with her heart so heavy she wondered if she would be charged an excess baggage fee. London greeted her with rain and dismal skies and when she called her flatmate, Jess, she found her room had been rented out to someone else.

'I'm so sorry, Izzy, but I thought you weren't coming back,' Jess said. 'What's happened? Where's Andrea?'

'We're not together any more,' Izzy said. 'I made a mistake. I shouldn't have married him. He doesn't love me.'

'Do you love him?' Jess's voice was soft with concern.

Izzy bit her lip to stop it from trembling. 'I'm an idiot for falling for someone like him. I don't know how it happened. One minute I hated him and the next...'

'But what will you do now? Doesn't this mean you lose your inheritance if you break up before the six months?'

'I don't care about the money,' Izzy said. 'Well, only a little bit.'

'Where will you live? I could put you up on the sofa for a night or two but—'

'It's all right. I'll find my own place. I'm not exactly destitute.' *Yet.*

Andrea arrived at his villa in Positano the following day with the expectation Izzy would be there once she'd had time to cool off. His hotel staff had told him she had left the hotel late but they had no idea of where she had gone. He'd done a quick ring around but hotel security was tight on giving out guest details, which was something he totally supported. But it was frustrating to spend the night pacing the floor with a host of ghastly scenarios flooding his brain. He'd tried calling her but her phone was switched off. He didn't leave a message because he wasn't sure what to say. *Come back, I need you* were not phrases he used. To anyone.

Gianna greeted him with her usual cheery smile

but her expression faded when she saw he was alone. 'Where's Izzy?'

'I was hoping she'd be here.' Andrea's stomach curdled anew with disappointment. A dark and bitter disappointment that yet again she had failed to do as he'd expected. As he'd hoped.

Gianna's dark brown eyes almost popped out of her head. 'Why didn't she come back with you? What's going on?'

'I'd rather not talk about it.'

'But where is she?'

Andrea strode past the housekeeper to go to his office. 'I don't want to be disturbed. Take the week off. Take a month off.'

He sat at his desk and stared at his computer screen. How had it come to this? He had been hoping Izzy would be back by now. He had given her twenty-four hours. How much longer did she need to see what a stupid thing she was doing? She was sabotaging her future. She was throwing away her chance of financial freedom. It was a ludicrous thing to do. No one in their right mind would walk away from that amount of money.

But money wasn't everything...

Andrea clenched his jaw until his teeth ached. Yes, it damn well was. Money might not buy happiness but it got you off the street. It got you out of the gutter and into a lifestyle that was the envy of others. It fed you and clothed you and transported you to places you'd only ever dreamed of as a child living in abject poverty.

He pushed back his chair and paced the floor until he was sure he would bald the carpet. He might have plenty of money but he had never felt so powerless. He was used to being in the driving seat of his life. He was the one who started and ended his relationships. He wasn't used to being left hanging, hoping for what he couldn't quite say. His pride had taken a hit. That was why he was feeling so out of sorts. What else could it be? He had been so sure Izzy wouldn't compromise her chance to inherit. She wanted her grandparents' house more than anything. He knew what it felt like to want something so badly nothing else mattered. Was she disappointed? Crushed that her dream of buying back that property was now out of her reach?

He went over to the window to look at the view from his office. The ocean sparkled below, the sun shone with brilliance and warmth but inside he felt cold and empty. He was like a king confined to his castle, surrounded by wealth and possessions that failed to deliver the contentment they had before.

Andrea rubbed a hand over his face and sighed. He needed to do something. Anything. Work was his panacea, wasn't it? The least he could do was buy the wretched property for her. Call him a sentimental fool but he couldn't stand by and let her miss out on that house. He sat back at his desk and searched online for the property details. Within an hour he had made an offer—way too generous, of course, and it would take a few days for a building inspection to be completed and a legal contract drawn up, but he wanted that property for Izzy and what he wanted he made it his business to get.

Well…mostly.

Work was what he needed to get back on form. Hard, relentless work. He had to stop thinking about Izzy and focus on something else. He needed to pour his frustrations into ticking off tasks. He was not going to let Izzy's desertion undo him. He hated to think what the press would make of their break-up once they heard about it.

But he was determined they wouldn't hear it via him.

Izzy found a temporary bedsit and a few days later hired a car and travelled down to take one last look at her grandparents' house. The day before she'd received a call from the owners to say a buyer had approached them and, due to the generosity of the offer, they'd felt compelled to sell rather than wait another few months. They were apologetic but pragmatic and Izzy could hardly blame them. She had been expecting such a call ever since she'd first hoped to buy the property. It was always going to be risky without having drawn up a legal agreement, but she hadn't been in the position to draw up anything.

She had just hoped. Vainly, foolishly, naïvely hoped.

But going down now to the house was her way of saying goodbye to the dream she'd had of reclaiming it. She'd heard nothing from Andrea since she'd arrived in London, although she had noticed a couple of missed calls the night she'd left Venice, but he hadn't left a message. She'd been bracing herself for the press to report on their failed relationship but so far there had been nothing. It was ironic to think of all the times in the past where she had courted scandal and now the sudden break-up of her marriage to Italy's most eligible bachelor had failed to rate a mention.

The country lane lined by hedgerows on the way to her grandparents' house brought a prickly lump to Izzy's throat. How many times had she been down this lane with Hamish by her side? Not enough. Nowhere near enough but those few precious memories were all she had left to treasure. Every field, every tree and wildflower were like old friends greeting

her. There was the old oak she had stood under and
watched in wonder as Hamish had built a tree house
specially for her. There was the little bridge over the
babbling stream that she and Hamish had walked
over on their way to his favourite fishing spot. There
was the copse of trees where they'd had a picnic and
he'd played hide and seek with her. She could almost
smell the fragrance of her grandmother's home-baked
treats, could almost hear the sound of her grandfa-
ther mowing the lawns on his ride-on mower because
he enjoyed the task so much even though there had
been a gardener.

This was where Izzy had felt closest to her mother
and she had hoped by reclaiming the house she would
somehow feel her mum would be proud of her.

The Georgian house finally came into view and
her heart stuttered when she saw the 'SOLD' notice
on an estate agent's sign by the entrance gates.

Izzy's shoulders slumped in defeat. So it really
was over. Even after the phone call from the owners she had still hoped it wasn't true. But it was true.
Her dream was destroyed. But strangely it didn't feel
as devastating as she'd thought. The house looked
tired and in need of some urgent attention. The garden was overgrown and the paintwork on the house
faded and even peeling in places. But even if the
house were beautifully restored, would she have been

happy without someone to share her vision of it with her? The only someone she wanted to share it with was Andrea and he didn't want to share his life with anyone, much less her.

It was just a house that had once been a happy place but the people who had made it happy were no longer there. But in a way they lived on in Izzy's heart. It was up to her now to honour her mother's and brother's and grandparents' memories by living a fully authentic life, not settling for second best or half measures.

Izzy turned the car around and drove back along the lane, leaving her childhood memories—and a little part of herself that would always belong there—behind.

A couple of days later Andrea received a package delivery by courier from Izzy containing the wedding and engagement rings and the jewellery he'd bought her. He sat in his office in Positano and stared at the diamonds and sapphires and wondered why she'd sent them back when she could have sold them. At least then she could have raised some funds to compensate for what she'd lost by bailing on their marriage. He searched through the packaging and found a handwritten note.

Dear Andrea,
I didn't feel comfortable keeping these any lon-
ger. I'll leave it to you to make the divorce ar-
rangements. Please say hello to Gianna for
me and apologise for how I left without saying
goodbye. I hope she understands.

By the way, my grandparents' house was
sold but I'm okay about it. It needs a lot of
work and I would never have been able to af-
ford it.
Izzy

Andrea stared at the note for a long moment. Why
was she leaving the divorce arrangements to him?
He picked up her wedding ring and suddenly realised he was still wearing his. Why hadn't he taken
it off? He let out a sigh that scraped at his throat like
a crab claw. He knew exactly why. It was the same
reason he'd gone to such trouble to buy her grandparents' property even though it would need hun-
dreds of thousands of pounds thrown at it to restore
it. As white elephants went it was a big one. It had
gone against every business principle he prided himself on but he'd felt compelled to at least make sure
she had something she wanted, even if it wasn't all
she'd hoped for. He'd been waiting for all the legal
work to be cleared up before he sent the deeds to

her. Maybe he should have contacted her before now but he didn't want her to think he was blackmailing her into coming back to him. The house was a gift. Wasn't it? Why else had he bought such a run-down sad excuse for a place?

But she didn't want possessions. She wanted love. Wasn't that what everyone wanted?

And yes, even him.

He'd been such a fool to let her go without a fight. He'd let her walk away because he hadn't had the guts to ask her to stay. He hadn't had the courage to admit to how he felt about her. He hadn't even recognised his feelings because for most of his life he'd been shut down emotionally. He had done the same thing to his mother. She had rejected him and he'd walked away without trying to understand what was going on for her. But he had already taken steps to fix things with his mother. He had Izzy to thank for showing him how blind he had been to his mother's point of view. It shamed him to think he had wasted all those years resenting his mother when he could have been helping her, protecting her.

But for now Izzy was his top priority—his only priority.

He had locked away his heart for fear of getting hurt and yet he had hurt Izzy. She hadn't told him she loved him but the signs were all there. He had to see her to tell her how he felt. He had to prove he was worthy of a second chance because he couldn't bear to live his life without her at the centre of it.

Izzy was in her bedsit, mindlessly watching a movie on her phone, when the doorbell rang. She used the term 'doorbell' loosely for it sounded more like a cat being slowly strangled than anything else. She clicked off her phone and answered the door, to find Andrea standing there carrying a package and a business-sized envelope. A sinkhole formed in her stomach. *The divorce papers.* He was bringing her the divorce papers to sign to activate proceedings. 'Hi,' she said, surprised her voice got past the lump in her throat. 'Won't you come in?'

He stepped through the doorway and closed the door behind him. 'How are you?' His voice had a gruff sound to it as if he'd swallowed something rough.

Izzy tried to smile but it didn't quite work. 'I'm fine. You?' Oh, God, how polite they both sounded. Like strangers. She glanced at the envelope in his hand and swallowed. 'Are those what I think they are?'

'What do you think they are?' Something about his expression made her wonder if he was smiling behind the screen of his shuttered gaze. How cruel of him to be amused at the end of their relationship.

But then, why wouldn't he be amused? He wasn't the one who would lose everything once they divorced.

'The divorce papers.' How it hurt for her to actually say those words out loud.

He passed the envelope to her. 'Why don't you open it and see if you're right?'

Izzy took the envelope with fingers that trembled. She broke the seal and pulled out the document, but it took her a moment to work out what it was. It was a legal document but it had nothing to do with a divorce. It was a property deed. The deed to her grandparents' property. She looked up at Andrea in puzzlement. 'I don't understand… Why are you giving me these?'

'It's yours, Izzy. The property is yours. I bought it for you.'

Izzy wasn't sure what had surprised her more—the fact he'd called her Izzy or his purchase of the property. 'I don't know what to say… I'm completely gobsmacked as to why you would do something like that.'

'Do you have no idea?' His eyes began to twinkle. 'No idea at all, *cara*?'

Izzy moistened her lips, which were suddenly drier than the document she was holding. She put the document down and looked at the other package he was carrying. 'W-what's in there?' Her voice stumbled over a budding hope.

He handed her the jewellery she'd sent back to him only a few days ago. 'I want you to put those rings back on, *cara*. I love you and I can't spend another day without you.'

Izzy opened and closed her mouth, her heart beating so fast she could almost hear it. 'You love me?'

He took her by the upper arms, his smile so tender it made her heart beat all the faster. 'I've been such a fool, *tesoro mio*. I can't believe I let you walk out of my life like that. I was so angry that you'd ended things that it took me a while to realise how I really felt. I love you so much. My life is so empty without you. All I do is work and mope around the place. Gianna is sick of me. She's threatening to resign. You have to put me out of my misery—and hers— and come back to me. Please? Forgive me for being a heartless brute in not telling you how I feel before now. I love you desperately.'

Izzy threw her arms around him and hugged him so tightly he grunted in pain. 'Oh, Andrea, I love you so much too. I can't believe how lonely and miserable I've been.'

He lifted her face so his gaze meshed with hers. 'You are the best thing that's ever happened to me. You make me feel alive in a way I've never felt before. I'm sorry we fought so much over the years. What were we thinking, wasting so much time?'

Relief at knowing he loved her as she loved him flooded Izzy like a powerful drug. A calming, healing drug that took away all the pain and sadness of the past. 'We'll make up for it in the future. No more fighting, only loving.'

He stroked his fingers across her cheek. 'The last few days have been torture, coming home to an empty house. Not seeing you. Not hearing your voice. Not sleeping beside you. I've missed you so much.'

Izzy smiled up at him, her gaze misty with happy tears. 'I've missed you so much too. I only realised how much I loved you at Patrizio and Elena's wedding. It made me feel so sad that our marriage hadn't been genuine. I hated our ceremony. It made me feel so cheap and disposable. I never want to feel like that again. Promise me we won't do that to each other.'

'We'll get married again,' Andrea said, holding her close. 'We'll have all the bells and whistles you like as long as you'll agree to be my wife for ever.'

Izzy gave him a teasing smile and linked her arms around his neck. 'I thought you didn't believe in forever love?'

He pressed a kiss to her mouth. 'I didn't until I fell in love with you. I want to grow old with you. I want to have babies with you. We can be a family, the sort of family both of us missed out on. You've taught me so much about love, my gorgeous girl. For all these years I've been blaming my mother, kicking me out on the street, but you got me thinking about her circumstances. I've managed to track her down and you were right. She sent me away because she was frightened my stepfather would kill me if I came back. She was terrified of him. I can't thank you enough for making me see how blind I was. It's still early days in rebuilding our relationship, but I want to buy her a nice house in a safe suburb. I also want to buy a house and turn it into a women's shelter. I'm hoping she'll let me name it after her to make up for my ignorance of her situation in the past.'

'Oh, darling, I'm so thrilled for you that you've got her back in your life,' Izzy said. 'You're such a good man. She must be so proud of who you've become. I was so against marriage before I met you because I was frightened I would end up with a marriage like my parents'. But you're nothing like my father. You make me feel like I'm worth something. You make me feel like a princess.' She couldn't stop some tears from falling from her eyes. 'You bought me that house not even knowing if I'd come back to you.'

Andrea took out a handkerchief and gently mopped her tears, his own eyes looking suspiciously moist. 'You are my world, Izzy. No amount of wealth I've accumulated over the years compares to you. When I thought I'd lost you I realised how little I care for possessions and status. I care only about you. You are my world and you are worth everything to me.'

'No one has ever said anything so wonderful to me before,' Izzy said, sniffing. 'I'm so happy I can't stop crying.'

He smiled and gathered her close. 'I hope I don't make you cry too often. I can't promise our life together will be perfect but I can promise I will be by your side no matter what. And this time, when we get married in church, do you know what I'm going to do when the priest says, "You may kiss the bride"?'

Izzy smiled back. 'What?'

His eyes glinted and his mouth came down to hers. 'I'm going to do this.' And then he kissed her.

* * * * *

If you enjoyed
Bound by a One-Night Vow
you're sure to enjoy these other stories
by Melanie Milburne!

The Tycoon's Marriage Deal
A Virgin for a Vow
Blackmailed into the Marriage Bed
Tycoon's Forbidden Cinderella

COMING NEXT MONTH FROM
HARLEQUIN
Presents.

Available October 16, 2018

#3665 THE ITALIAN'S CHRISTMAS HOUSEKEEPER
by Sharon Kendrick

When shy Molly is found sobbing by Salvio, he comforts her...with the most amazing experience of her life. But when it costs Molly her job, she must become Salvio's temporary housekeeper—just in time for Christmas!

#3666 THE BABY THE BILLIONAIRE DEMANDS
Secret Heirs of Billionaires
by Jennie Lucas

When Rodrigo discovers Lola's secret, he's determined his child will take his name! Their desire is undeniable, and Lola will show Rodrigo that their son—and their connection—is worth fighting for!

#3667 THE INNOCENT'S SHOCK PREGNANCY
One Night With Consequences
by Carol Marinelli

Wherever Ethan goes, the press follow. So when he discovers his night with Merida ended in pregnancy, he moves fast to contain the scandal! Suddenly, Merida is playing the part of the loving Mrs. Deveraux...

#3668 SHEIKH'S SECRET LOVE-CHILD
Bound to the Desert King
by Caitlin Crews

Sheikh Malak assumed he'd never inherit the throne, but when his brother unexpectedly abdicates, he finds himself king! Now past indiscretions must be put aside. Until he uncovers the hidden consequence of one delicious seduction...

#3669 SICILIAN'S BRIDE FOR A PRICE
Conveniently Wed!
by Tara Pammi

To counter a business threat, ruthless Dante must get married! Free-spirited Alisha will do anything to save her mother's charity—even marry Dante. But the price of their marriage is more than they bargained for...

#3670 HER FORGOTTEN LOVER'S HEIR
by Annie West

Pietro is stunned to learn Molly is pregnant—but an accident leaves Molly with no memory of him! Pietro must help Molly remember their fierce attraction, and the fact that the baby she's carrying is the Agosti heir...

#3671 REVENGE AT THE ALTAR
by Louise Fuller

Nothing gives Max more satisfaction than hearing Margot say "I do." Though he was rejected by her family once before, this time, Max holds all the cards! But their wedding night tempts Max to forget revenge...

#3672 A RING TO CLAIM HIS LEGACY
by Rachael Thomas

Marco can't forget the woman he spent a week with on a luxurious island. So when he learns she's expecting his baby, he's convinced their child will secure his family's dynasty...

*When shy Molly is found sobbing by Salvio, he comforts
her…with the most amazing experience of her life. But
when it costs Molly her job, she must become Salvio's
temporary housekeeper—just in time for Christmas!*

*Read on for a sneak preview of
Sharon Kendrick's next story,*
The Italian's Christmas Housekeeper.

"The only thing that will stop me is you," he continued,
his voice a deep silken purr. "So stop me, Molly. Turn
away and walk out right now and do us both a favor,
because something tells me this is a bad idea."

He was giving her the opportunity to leave but Molly
knew she wasn't going to take it—because when did
things like this ever happen to people like her? She
wasn't like most women her age. She'd never had sex.
Never come even close, despite her few forays onto a
dating website that had all ended in disaster. Yet now
a man she barely knew was proposing seduction and
suddenly she was up for it, and she didn't care if it was
bad. Hadn't she spent her whole life trying to be good?
And where had it gotten her?

Her heart was crashing against her rib cage as she stared up into his rugged features and greedily drank them in. "I don't care if it's a bad idea," she whispered. "Maybe I want it as much as you do."

Don't miss
The Italian's Christmas Housekeeper,
available November 2018 wherever
Harlequin Presents® books and ebooks are sold.

www.Harlequin.com